Disarming Detective

ELIZABETH HEITER

First published in Great Britain 2015
by Mills & Boon, an imprint of Harlequin (UK) Limited,
Large Print edition 2015
Eton House, 18-24 Paradise Road,
Richmond, Surrey, TW9 1SR

© 2015 Elizabeth Heiter

ISBN: 978-0-263-26012-0

Harlequin (UK) Limited's policy is to use papers that are natural, renewable and recyclable products and made from wood grown in sustainable forests. The logging and manufacturing processes conform to the legal environmental regulations of the country of origin.

Printed and bound in Great Britain
by CPI Antony Rowe, Chippenham, Wiltshire

She gave him a sassy smile. "I'm armed.

"And," she continued, "the Bureau believes pretty strongly in teaching its agents defensive training. Believe me, I got the bruises to prove it back at the Academy, but I learned. This guy won't want to mess with me."

Logan didn't seem any less worried. "I'd still feel better if you were somewhere else. You can stay with me if you want. I have an extra bedroom."

Her nerve endings tingled at the idea, but Ella forced herself to give him a look of disbelief. "Yeah, because that would really work." If she stayed at his house, she'd end up in his bed, and they both knew it. Appealing as it might sound, that idea had *heartbreak* written all over it. And she didn't have time to mess around.

She was here to catch a killer.

ELIZABETH HEITER

likes her suspense to feature strong heroines, chilling villains, psychological twists and a little romance. Her research has taken her into the minds of serial killers, through murder investigations and onto the FBI Academy's shooting range. Elizabeth graduated from the University of Michigan with a degree in English literature. She's a member of International Thriller Writers and Romance Writers of America. Visit Elizabeth at www.elizabethheiter.com

Acknowledgments

I'd like to thank my family and friends
for supporting me while I get lost in novel
writing and deadlines. Thank you for
sharing my excitement about every sale
and every book event and every bit of
good news. And thank you
for reminding me to come out of
my writing cave every once in a while.

My own personal version of the
usual suspects: Chris Heiter,
Robbie Terman, Ann Forsaith,
Nora Smith, Charles Shipps,
Sasha Orr, Mark Nalbach,
Caroline Heiter and Kathryn Merhar.
You know why your names show up in
every acknowledgment, and I hope you
know how much I appreciate you!

Finally, to my agent, Kevan Lyon,
and my editor, Paula Eykelhof.
You are the kind of team every writer
dreams of working with—thank you
for making my dreams come true!

Chapter One

The instant Isabella Cortez left the safety of the FBI building, goose bumps skittered across her skin and her senses went on high alert. Her instincts and training, like a sudden alarm shrieking inside her head, told her she wasn't alone.

The door slammed shut behind her before she could dart back inside, and Ella cursed the heavy briefcase weighing down one hand and the stack of file folders clenched in the other. Just because she was taking her first real vacation in two years didn't mean killers took time off, so her cases were coming with her. Assuming she made it to her vacation.

Tonight, she was the last one out of the bland

office building in Aquia, Virginia. It was set back off the road, nestled deep in the woods, and manned by an armed guard. Entrance to the parking lot was supposed to be reserved for the FBI's Criminal Investigative Analysts who worked there and no one else. If a visitor was arriving, the guard at the gate called ahead. Anyone who could make it past security was a threat.

Pushing back her fear, she blinked, trying to adjust to the darkness outside. Her arms tensed, but she didn't drop the files and reach for her gun. Not yet. Not until she identified the threat. If she acted too soon, she'd probably get shot.

No, all the instincts honed by two years in the Behavioral Analysis Unit told her to let him think she was oblivious. Let him show himself before she brought him down.

Her heart thudded too fast, reminding Ella all too clearly of her first years in the FBI, in the gangs unit in Dallas, when she'd taken a bullet to the leg and her partner had taken two to the chest. At the memory, all the nerves in her leg burst to life, painful and fire-poker hot.

Lock it down, Cortez. Focus.

A tiny movement made her glance left, toward the only two cars in the lot. A bulky figure shifted beside her car, stepping into the dim glow of the overhead light.

He was big, taller than her by half a foot and outweighing her by a good fifty pounds and all of it muscle. But none of that mattered if she didn't let him get close.

Her eyes darted to his hands. Empty. She let out a breath, but it caught when she spotted the telltale bulge at his hip. No way was she giving him a chance to go for the weapon. She dropped her briefcase and files fast, yanking her Glock pistol from its holster. "Hands up!"

"Whoa!" He lifted his hands near his head. "Look, I—"

"Higher. Get on your knees."

"Hey, I didn't—"

"Now!" Ella took a step closer, let him see the

dead seriousness in her eyes, the solid, steady aim of her gun. "Pull your weapon out with your left hand. Toss it over here."

"Crap." He complied, getting on his knees and sending his own Glock skidding across the pavement toward her.

"You have any other weapons on you?"

"No. Look, I'm a homicide detective. I flew up here from Florida to talk to a profiler."

She narrowed her eyes, noting the slight Southern drawl in his voice now that she wasn't laser-focused on containing him. "How'd you get in here?"

"The guard let me in. My badge is in my pocket, okay?"

Ella frowned. With the regular guard on maternity leave, maybe the newbie had broken protocol. "Fine. Toss it to me with your wallet."

He let out a breath through his nose, something like amusement in his voice. "Wow, you're thorough."

He was right about that. At the BAU, her job

was to create criminal personality profiles of the country's most depraved killers. Every day, her work told her what one inattentive moment, one second of blind trust, could cost.

It was a lesson she'd first learned nearly ten years ago, when her best friend had been violently attacked. It had introduced Ella to a kind of evil she'd never known existed, and completely altered the path of her life. Now, viewing everyone as a potential threat seemed almost normal.

He tossed his wallet and badge over, but even before she picked it up, she knew it was the real thing. Still keeping her weapon leveled on him—mostly for scaring the crap out of her and making her dump her case files all over the ground—she flipped open the wallet to his ID. The face staring back at her, with its hard lines and no-nonsense stare, looked every bit a homicide detective. "Logan Greer. Oakville, Florida."

Reholstering her weapon underneath her

blazer, she tossed the wallet back and tried to slow her heart rate to normal speed. "Way to make an impression, Greer."

He gave her a smile full of self-deprecating humor that made her realize again that the bulky size that had unnerved her in the darkness was impressive muscle tone, that beneath the piercing stare were moss green eyes. She was a sucker for green eyes. Too bad she hadn't run into him on the beach next week with a margarita in her hand instead of on her last day before vacation, toting a gun.

As he gathered his badge and weapon, Logan asked, "And you are…?"

Ella brushed her bangs out of her eyes and extended her hand. "Special Agent Ella Cortez, BAU."

"Perfect," Logan said, giving her another hit of that one-sided grin as he took his time shaking her hand. "Because I need a profiler to look at my homicide case."

Ella pulled her hand free and collected the

files scattered on the pavement. "You're gonna have to go through channels."

"I did that." When she started to walk past him, he put a hand on her arm. "Please. Look, they wouldn't assign anyone to it."

Ella sighed, frustration warring with sympathy. He'd flown here for help and she knew if her boss had already refused, he would get shut down again. Getting a profiler assigned meant that the case needed one. The most likely reason Logan hadn't gotten help was because he had a case where the killer would logically come up without resorting to a profile.

She couldn't take this on even if she weren't about to leave on vacation. Even if she were allowed to pick her own cases. She already had more files stacked up than she could possibly handle with the attention they needed in her regular ten-hour days.

"Sorry." Ella didn't look at him as she dumped her briefcase and files in the trunk of her car.

"How is your office supposed to know

whether I have a serial killer from a one page form?" There was frustration in Logan's voice, but steel underneath. "I'll wait as long as I have to, but I need help on this."

"I'm the last one out. Everyone else has already gone home."

He stepped around in front of her, leaning against her car between her and the driver's door, his arms crossed loosely over his chest. "I'll wait here until tomorrow if I have to. But wouldn't it be easier for everyone if you took a look? Please, just hear me out. An hour of your time. That's all I'm asking. Just take a look at my case file. Give me *something* I can take home and use, before the bodies start piling up."

When she heaved out a sigh and looked up, he shot her a determined stare, as if he could get her to agree through force of will alone. She stared back into his imploring green eyes, which were close enough that she could see little flecks of gold around the edges of his irises.

She didn't have time for this. And she needed

to get away from case file after case file of vicious murders. She needed those two weeks at the beach with her two best friends, while they all tried to distract themselves from the anniversary coming up too fast, the one they all wanted to forget.

She needed to have dinner, then pack and make her way to the airport. Of course, three weeks of late nights trying to get ahead of work before taking time off meant her refrigerator was stocked only with condiments. She looked into Logan Greer's green eyes and heard herself say, "Tell you what. You can buy me dinner and while we eat, I'll look at your case."

The genuinely grateful smile he flashed her sent unexpected shivers of awareness over her skin that reminded her she hadn't had a date in months. Another casualty of the job.

Wow, she *really* needed this vacation.

"TEN O'CLOCK IS a little late for dinner. Is the FBI opposed to meal breaks?" Logan asked, one eyebrow quirked, as she scarfed down French fries as if she hadn't seen food in weeks.

In the light of the little diner, which Ella frequented because it reminded her of something she'd find back home in Indiana, Logan looked a lot less like a potential threat and a lot more like the kind of guy she'd try to flirt with in the grocery store. The kind of guy she'd be tempted to chase after, no matter how it would inevitably end.

Wearing jeans and a faded gray T-shirt, with a five-o'clock shadow heavy on his chin, he looked exactly like her type. Laid-back attitude, but intensity in his eyes. Masculine, but judging by the easy way he was teasing her half an hour after she pulled her gun on him, secure enough not to find her intimidating.

Of course, that was her initial read on him. Given that her longest relationship in the past had lasted a whole five months, she'd decided she was far better at profiling murderers than potential dates. Not that Logan Greer was a potential for anything except being easy on the eyes while she helped him with his case.

"You're the one who showed up late at night expecting someone to be there."

"I came straight from the airport. And you weren't the first profiler I harassed in the parking lot. You're just the first one who succumbed to my charm."

Ella snorted. The agent out the door before her had been Jack Reid, perpetually in a foul mood and perpetually using a foul mouth. "You mean Jack didn't invite you out to dinner?"

"Well, he invited me to do something. But it sounded anatomically impossible."

"Probably a come-on," Ella joked, then feigned hurt as she stuffed another fry, heavily coated with ketchup, in her mouth. "So, you're telling me I wasn't your first choice?"

Logan's gaze shifted appreciatively over her, lingering on her mouth. Then he gave her steady eye contact, let her see an interest that went beyond the case. "Believe me, if I'd known *you* were coming, I would have waited."

Ella rolled her eyes, even as she willed her cheeks not to heat. This never happened to her, this instant, powerful lure to a man she'd just met, let alone to one she'd just pulled a gun on. "I was trying to get caught up on some work before I left town." She held out a hand, palm up. Back to business. "You have a case file?"

He set a thin manila folder in her palm, his big calloused hand brushing hers. "Where are you going?"

"Vacation with some friends. I plan to sit on the beach and do nothing more strenuous than put on sunscreen." Of course, that would last about a day and then she'd be searching for kayak rentals or somewhere to take surfing lessons. Sitting still wasn't her strong suit.

"I don't suppose you're coming to Florida? Because I'm willing to help you out with the sunscreen."

One of the cases in the trunk of her car—the

only one she hadn't actually been assigned—
was from Florida. No, she and her two best
friends were heading as far from Florida as possible. "California, actually."

"Too bad. Other than the recent murder,
Oakville is a pretty nice place to visit."

Ella blinked, so surprised to hear real disappointment in his tone that she almost missed
the part about the case. "Wait a minute. Murder? Not murders?" No wonder her boss hadn't
assigned an agent to create a profile. Well, this
was going to be a quick dinner. At least she'd
be able to put Logan's mind at ease and hopefully point him in the right direction. One kill
probably meant the perpetrator had been in the
victim's life.

"Yeah, I know. One murder doesn't make a
serial killer. I get it." He leaned forward. "But
look at the file, okay? This isn't a first kill. We
got lucky, finding this body. There are more.
I'm sure of it."

"Why?"

"The kill was too perfect. I don't think it was someone she knew, and the evidence is so slim. The fact that we even have a body—that we even know she's dead—is a fluke. We don't have a lot of murders in Oakville, but a killer just doesn't get that good without practice."

Logan frowned. The attraction he'd been broadcasting since they'd arrived at the diner was still in his eyes, but now it was tempered, pushed behind a sudden seriousness telling her he'd do whatever it took to find this killer.

Ella didn't need to see him work to believe it. She knew he was a good detective. It was there in the doggedness of his stare, in the trust he put in his instincts, in the way he was chasing this lead with all he had.

But she also saw this was more than just another case to him. He'd flown all this way for help, probably on his own dime. "You knew the victim, didn't you?"

"Jeez, you're good. I didn't know her well. But she was a friend of my sister's. Visiting from out of state. She'd actually left for the airport and we assumed she was back home." His lips tightened into a hard, thin line. "When all along, she was in Oakville. We found her in the marsh. Well, what was left of her anyway. We've got gators in the marshes, which is why I say we got lucky. Why I think there are more victims—because that's a pretty genius way to destroy evidence."

Ella nodded, flipping open the file folder next to her sandwich. The sight that greeted her should have made her lose her appetite, but she'd long ago learned to eat while reviewing case files. "Doesn't look like you had much to work with at the autopsy."

When she glanced up at Logan, he was carefully not looking at the photo and she reminded herself he knew the woman. She flipped past the autopsy photos, folded her hands under her chin and leaned toward him. "Why don't you give me the highlights?"

Logan raked a hand through his dark, close-cropped hair and she noticed the shadows under his eyes, the weariness lurking underneath those quick smiles.

"The victim was Theresa Crowley. My sister's age—twenty-five."

She must have looked surprised, because he said, "Yeah, Becky's ten years younger than I am. My parents didn't think they could have any more kids after me. Anyway, Theresa was a friend of Becky's from college. She lived in Arkansas. Flew in to visit for a week. She left as scheduled and my sister assumed she was already home until we identified the body."

"Who found her?"

"Local fisherman. He pulled out the remains and brought her in by boat."

Ella realized she was gaping as Logan continued, "Yeah, I know. Not great for evidence, but better than not having a body at all because the alligators finished her off."

"How long was she missing?"

"She left for the airport early Sunday morning and her body was found Monday afternoon."

"Short window to run into a killer."

"Unless he'd already been stalking her," Logan argued.

"What makes you think it wasn't someone she knew? Statistically, that's much more likely."

"Yeah, believe me, I don't run to the FBI every time we get a murder, whether or not I know the victim. But who did she know in Oakville? My sister and some of our family. That's it. Her rental car turned up the next day, abandoned in a mall parking lot a few towns over, in the opposite direction from the airport."

Ella sighed and set down her milkshake. "Are you sure you should be on this case?"

"Why? Because my family are obvious suspects?"

Instead of agreeing, Ella said, "Because you knew her."

"Another detective on the force already cleared

my family. It was pretty easy. We were at a town function at her time of death."

Ella stared at him, looking for any tiny twitch that would tell her he knew—or suspected— his family could be involved. All she saw was his determination to get her to help. And that heavy dose of attraction. Her heart rate picked up and she glanced down at her food before she gave anything away. "She have any obvious enemies?"

"Stalker exes, that kind of thing? No."

"Sexual assault?"

Logan shrugged. "My guess would be yes, but too much postmortem damage to tell for sure. She died from lack of oxygen, but there was no water in her lungs. She didn't drown in that marsh. She was killed somewhere else."

"Okay—"

"And she had burns on her body."

Ella felt her hands tense into fists. Hiding them under the table, she forced them to loosen. "What kind of burns?"

"What were they made with? I don't know. But she had several. On her arm, her back..." Fury pulsated in his voice. "Someone burned her on purpose."

Ella held back a string of curses. Burns were close enough to branding that those cases hit her hardest. She always wanted them and her boss, knowing why she'd joined the FBI six years ago, always passed them on to another agent.

As much as she hated it, she understood that he was right. She made them too personal, and getting too close to a case meant making mistakes. Like Logan was in danger of doing right now.

She gave him her best profiler stare, the one she'd learned from her boss—a legend in the Bureau. "I'm going to read this case file and give you my best insight. But I'm going to tell you something you already know. You're too close to this case. You shouldn't be on it."

It was hypocritical advice, given the very, very personal case file sitting in the trunk of her Bureau-issued car right now, and judging by his scowl, Logan didn't seem any more inclined to follow it than she was.

"I'm not handing this over to someone else, not when everyone seems to think it was a fluke. I'm not going to sit around and wait for the next body to show up before I investigate this. This was my sister's friend and someone murdered her and tossed her in the marsh like garbage. I'm going to find this guy and make sure he pays."

Realization struck Ella. "You're not supposed to be here, are you?"

Logan let out a sound that was half laugh, half exasperation, but his face told her he was impressed. "Tell you what, profiler. Check out the file and tell me I'm wrong." He gave her a smug look that said, "I dare you."

Ella nodded slowly. "Okay." She skipped over the autopsy photos and started reading. The further she got in the file, the more she felt her mouth tug downward.

When she looked back up at him, Logan raised his eyebrows. "Well?"

"You've got good instincts, Greer."

Logan tapped his fingers heavily on the table. "I thought so."

She had just flipped the file back to the beginning when he suggested, this time sounding completely serious, "Maybe you and your friends could vacation on some Florida beaches instead."

"No." The word came out more harshly than she'd intended, so she covered up her instant reaction by tilting her head and offering him an exaggerated coy smile. "Are you trying to solve a case here or get into my pants, Greer?"

He blinked and leaned back, but just as quickly sat forward with a full-wattage version of the smile he'd been laying on her all night. "Is it too much to hope for both?"

A short burst of laughter escaped her lips as desire zinged through her body. "Probably." She turned back to the file and all humor and lust instantly fled.

She lifted the page closer, squinting at one of the close-ups underneath the main autopsy photo, and her entire body suddenly felt as though it had been submerged in ice. The blood left her head so fast she actually swayed in her seat.

From a great distance, she heard Logan saying, "Whoa. Are you okay?" and before she knew it, he was squeezed in next to her in the booth, his hand on her back like fire against the frost that had come over her. "Ella?"

"What is this?"

Logan studied her face with concern before looking down. "The burn on her neck?"

"Yeah." She thought of marshes and fishermen. And images of hooks, burned into human flesh. "Could it be a brand?"

His forehead creased and he was staring into her eyes again, searching.

This close, he'd be able to see too much. Fear, maybe. Pain, probably. Recognition, definitely.

She'd seen a mark like this before, way too up close and personal. Her friend had covered it with a tattoo, but Ella would never forget how it had looked the day Maggie stumbled home to their dorm room. An angry red permanent reminder of a man the media had dubbed the Fishhook Rapist. He'd started with Maggie nearly a decade ago, then claimed a new victim every year since in a different part of the country. His last victim had been in Florida.

Ella had joined the FBI to catch him. She'd never even come close before. But maybe—just maybe—that was about to change.

"I don't know," Logan answered. "It's possible. Why?"

Ella released her breath, tried to regain control as she slapped the file shut. "I'm coming to Florida."

Chapter Two

There was definitely something about this case Ella Cortez wasn't telling him.

The bustle of Dulles Airport seemed to fade into the background as Logan watched her walk toward him, carrying two cups of coffee. A Bureau blue duffel bag was slung easily over one shoulder and it bounced against her hip with every purposeful stride, swinging in a hypnotic arc. More than one man's head swiveled as she passed.

Logan had come directly to the airport to change his flight and book hers, while she'd gone home to pack. And apparently to change. Instead of the all-business suit she'd had on earlier, now she wore jeans and a T-shirt that high-lighted appealing curves. Dark hair that had been wound into a bun earlier was now in a loose, low ponytail that trailed to midback and made his fingers itch to slide through it.

He sat up straighter as she joined him, taking the scalding cup of coffee she offered. "Thanks."

"Sure." She looked distracted as she dumped her bag on the floor, pulled out her cell phone and hit Redial. It must have gone to voice mail, because she swore and stuck the phone back in her pocket.

"Boyfriend?" When she squinted at him, he added, "That you're calling?"

"No. The friends I was supposed to go on vacation with. I can't get them."

Which didn't exactly answer the subtext of his question. Not that it mattered.

He'd gotten a lot more than he'd hoped for out of his trip, which he'd booked yesterday on a whim and a hope. He'd expected to badger someone from the FBI's profiler unit into giving him something to take home. It was how he got to the bottom of most of his cases—his ability to push until he got what he wanted. And this time wasn't any different. He wanted to close this case. And it didn't matter whose toes he had to step on back home.

He snuck a peek at Ella, who was frowning beside him as she pulled her phone out again. However much he'd like to believe it, she wasn't here because of his persuasive charm. She was in this for her own reasons. And before they landed, he planned to find out what they were.

"Ella!"

The yell jolted Ella to her feet. She hadn't made it two steps before a man and woman reached her. "I tried to call you," the man said.

He was tall, with a sharp, intent look that pegged him as law enforcement or military. He seemed to buzz with energy, and every-thing about him screamed his readiness for a vacation. Logan could read his type instantly—lady killer. Ella had called him a friend, but was that all?

The woman with him was dark-haired and muscular, with pretty blue eyes. She looked exhausted, frazzled and slightly jumpy.

"You're at the wrong gate." The man's eyes flicked speculatively to him, then back to Ella. "We're at the end of the terminal."

Ella bit her lip. "I can't make it."

"What?" The man's eyebrows shot up. "What do you mean?"

Logan got to his feet, which made her friends glance his way.

Ella's words suddenly doubled in speed. "This is Logan Greer. I have to help him with a case." She slowed down to add, "Logan, these are my friends, Maggie and Scott Delacorte."

Logan smiled. Well, that answered his question about Ella's relationship with Scott, if he was married to her friend Maggie. "Nice to meet you."

Maggie gave him a nod while Scott studied him with narrowed eyes before saying, "You, too."

"The three of us grew up together," Ella continued, still talking fast, as if trying to keep her friends from returning to the previous subject. "Maggie and Scott lived down the street from me. I probably spent as much time at their house as my own."

It took Logan a few seconds too long to deconstruct her words and realize Maggie and Scott weren't married, but brother and sister. By the time he'd figured out a response, Scott had turned to Ella again.

"You have a case?" Scott pushed. "You're supposed to have two weeks of vacation. We planned this months ago."

Ella's whole face twitched as she told them, "I don't have a choice. My boss made me cancel. If I can wrap it up fast, I'll fly out and join you."

Logan tried not to let his surprise at her lie show on his face, but from the way Scott squinted at first Ella, then him, he was pretty sure he'd failed.

Maggie, though, must not have noticed. Bloodshot eyes full of disappointment locked on Ella's. "There has to be someone else who can take the case."

Ella couldn't seem to hold Maggie's gaze as she said, "I'm sorry."

Just as boarding for their flight was announced, Scott's hand closed around Ella's arm, pulling her off to the side. It was probably to keep him from overhearing, but Scott's voice was too loud when he asked, "Can't you get your boss to reassign it? Did you tell him..."

Scott glanced back and Logan figured it was at him until Maggie sighed. "Let it go, Scott. She'll fly out if she can."

The scowl lurking on Scott's face shifted to resignation as he gave Ella a quick hug. "Okay. I guess you can't refuse orders. Good luck with the case. Wrap it up fast and join us, all right?"

Maggie hugged Ella with a barely audible, "Don't worry about it," and then she was shaking Logan's hand with surprising strength. "Which field office are you out of, Logan?"

"I'm—"

Ella jumped in. "Logan's not Bureau. And he's got a case down South I'm going to help him with. Hopefully, it'll be quick and then I'll grab a flight to California."

Her answer brought more questioning looks from Scott, but then final boarding for their flight was called and Ella grabbed her bag, looking relieved.

Logan waited until they were belted into their seats in the last row of the small plane and the doors were closed. "Are you planning to let me in on the big secret?"

"I don't know what you mean."

"Okay. What I mean is, why did you tell your friends you were assigned the case and couldn't get out of it?"

She turned sideways to face him, her knee

jabbing his thigh, and raised an eyebrow. "You want me to get out of it?"

Logan grinned as the engines started up. "It's a little late to change your mind now."

Ella leaned back in her seat. "This vacation was kind of a big deal. I didn't want to tell them I'd taken the case unofficially."

She was extremely close to Maggie and Scott, that was easy to see. And from the way she'd twitched and changed the subject as fast as she could in the airport, it was clear she rarely lied to them. Which meant that whatever she'd seen in the case file, whatever had persuaded her to come to Florida, was big. "So, why did you take the case?"

"Why? Because you were right about having a serial killer. Because you need a profile. And because it didn't seem like you were about to get one from anyone else."

"That's why you took the case?"

She shot him a look full of exasperation, color rising high in her cheeks. "Yes."

"You want to try that again?"

She looked sideways at him. "Okay, fine. There's a chance it could be connected to something I've seen before."

She held up a hand to forestall any argument, but he'd been focused more on the movement of her lips than her words, so by the time his brain caught up, she'd moved on.

"If it looks like it really is connected, I'll tell you about it. Until then, we need to focus on this victim."

"If you're here because it might be connected, shouldn't we look at the old case, too, so we don't miss anything?"

"No."

Ella turned to face him, bringing her knee back into contact with his thigh and sending his mind way off track. Jeez, he either really needed a date other than the ones his well-meaning family set up for him, or Ella Cortez was going to be a distraction. One he'd better learn to ignore. And fast.

"If it's not the same perp, we could just go in the wrong direction," Ella said.

"So, what's it going to take for you to decide if these cases are connected and let me in on the secret?"

Her lips tightened but her tone was calm when she replied, "Trust me. I'm good at what I do. I'll tell you if you need to know."

Any answer that included the words *need to know* sounded suspicious to him, but she was the expert. And since her consultation was unofficial and she could leave whenever she wanted, he decided he'd take what he could get. At least for now.

The direction he was taking in the investigation wasn't exactly sanctioned, so he couldn't fault her for having her own motivation. Especially since she'd soon see just how far off the approved path he'd veered.

He leaned back against the headrest and closed his eyes as the plane bounced up and down and then plummeted briefly as if it was aspiring to be a roller coaster. "I guess we all have our secrets."

As soon as Logan walked through the door of the Blue Dolphin, he could tell he'd made a mistake. But Ella had already gone in, so he let the door close behind him and followed through the crush of tourists and locals, through the smell of sunscreen and salt water.

Having lived in Oakville all his life, Logan knew a lot of the locals. If he hadn't, he would have been able to separate them from the tourists by dress alone. The locals all wore layers in deference to the heat outside and the air-conditioning blasting inside. Most of them, acclimatized to much warmer weather come summer, were still in pants. The tourists sported flip-flops, cutoffs and tiny bathing suit tops, their wet hair still dripping from the nearby ocean.

Crammed around a table near the front of the deli were four uniforms who'd set their sandwiches down as soon as they saw him. He watched the smiles quiver at the edges of their lips, the laughter dance in their eyes, and knew what was coming.

Hank O'Connor was senior in the group, nearly as big across as he was tall. He gave his companions a nod, an unspoken "watch this," then called out, "Hey Greer, catch your serial killer yet?"

The rest of the table snickered, and Ella stopped staring at the menu above the counter long enough to glance questioningly from the uniforms to Logan.

"I'm working on it, O'Connor," Logan threw back. "How about you? Catch any speeders today?"

The smile dropped off Hank's face. They'd taken the detective exam at the same time. They'd both passed, but only one job had opened up and since Logan had been there longer, with more experience, procedure dictated that he got it. Hank was about as happy with Logan's position as the chief was.

Hank jerked a little straighter in his seat and Logan knew he should just have let it go. Hank had a bad temper, a long memory and a penchant for petty revenge.

"Not everybody's daddy can buy them a job," Hank spat.

As one, the cops with Hank went for their sandwiches again, their eyes cast downward.

Familiar frustration filled Logan, threatening to overflow, but he clenched his teeth and turned back to the counter. He'd fought this battle too many times to bother.

Yes, his family had a long history in Oakville. Yes, his father, the mayor, had been in office for years. Admittedly, it had given him some advantages in his life. But when it came to his career, it always seemed to be a disadvantage. Because no matter how hard he worked, there was always someone anxious to claim he was just trading on the Greer name.

"Your family were the last ones to see the Crowley girl, right?" Hank pressed. "You spinning your serial killer story so nobody brings *that* up in the next election?"

Logan's fingers curled into his palms as he spun back toward Hank, acid on his tongue.

With a speed he wouldn't have expected from a desk jockey profiler, Ella ducked in front of him and held her hand out toward the table of cops with an overly cheery smile. "Officer O'Connor, is it? I'm Special Agent Ella Cortez, FBI. I'm here because Detective Greer's serial killer theory looks promising."

Hank engulfed Ella's hand in his own bear paw and shook it a few times, a startled expression on his face. His mouth opened and closed, but no words emerged. His companions looked at each other with equal surprise.

Before they could recover, Ella grabbed Logan's arm and steered him back toward the counter, ordering herself a sandwich. Logan fought his laughter until they were both out the door and back in his Chevy Caprice with their food.

But any urge to laugh faded as he drove toward the marsh. Knowing Hank, both the fact that Logan was still pursuing the serial killer angle and the fact that he now had a cute FBI profiler in tow would make it back to his chief before the end of the day. Which would lead to a conversation that he had hoped to avoid a little longer.

Swallowing a sigh, Logan eased his unmarked police vehicle off the side of the road as close to the marsh as they were going to get. "We're hoofing it from here," he told Ella.

She stuffed the last bite of her sandwich in her mouth and got out of the car, drawing a deep breath that told him she wasn't used to the heavy humidity. "I thought we were going to the marsh?"

"We are." They were standing off the side of the road, bracketed by hundred-year-old live oaks. Spanish moss dangled from every branch almost to the tall grass below, like a fuzzy gray curtain obscuring the path behind it. "Follow me. And stay on the trail. Snakes hide in the grass."

Behind the trees, the dirt path was packed down. Locals used it often to bike and walk or to get to the marshes for fishing. Right now, in the midday heat, the path was empty.

It was also narrow, so Ella walked behind him. He could sense her taking in the details, so he wasn't surprised when she asked, "Is the area we're going to pretty populated?"

"We definitely get locals looking for redfish, but not too many tourists wander back here. We won't get out as far as where the body was found. To do that, we'd need a boat. The trail loops back around, which is where most of the runners take it, but there's a split that goes farther out, about to the point the water will come up to at high tide. From there, I can show you where we found Theresa." He glanced over his shoulder at her. "You're wondering if this guy knew the area in order to get back here?"

"That's part of it. Also trying to determine

how likely it is he'd run into other people. How much risk he'd take dumping the body where he did. Things like that help me figure out his personality."

"Hmm." Logan dropped back so he could walk beside her and watch her face as she talked. They were a close fit on the narrow trail. Every few steps her arm brushed his and the feel of her skin fired way too many nerve endings to life. "From what I know of profiling, you'll be able to tell me things like he's a white male in his twenties."

From the reaction he'd gotten when he'd suggested bringing in a profiler to his chief, he knew skeptics joked that was all profilers were good for—looking at a crime scene and predicting that the serial killer was a white male in his twenties. Which happened to be the most common age range and race for serial killers.

Ella's mouth quirked, but with annoyance or amusement, he couldn't tell.

"The basic concepts behind profiling are actually pretty simple," she said. "Take you, for example. Things like your upbringing, your intelligence, your personality—all of that contributed to why you became not just a cop, but a homicide detective. Creating a criminal personality profile analyzes that. I look at the evidence—things like the way he dumped the body—and figure out details of his personality. From that, I can say what kind of job that kind of personality would likely pick, what kind of environment he'd live in, if he'd be married, that sort of thing." She shrugged. "Make sense?"

"You make it sound easy."

"No, it's definitely not easy. But it is pretty grounded in psychology." As they reached the end of the trail, she turned to face him, and he instantly became hyperaware of how short the distance between them really was. "If I tell you he's a white male in his twenties, there'll be a reason behind it besides averages."

Turning again, she squinted out over the marsh, her expression slipping back to serious, and after allowing himself another few seconds to watch her, Logan did the same.

He'd been to this spot hundreds of times before, but in the sudden stillness, he saw it as she might. The feeling of intense calm that came from being the only people there, then the slow realization that nature was moving all around. The murky waters, lapping against tall grasses. The curious expression of a wading egret, the distant lump indicating an alligator underneath.

"It's pretty quiet," Ella said.

He could almost hear her thoughts, calculating details about the killer. He'd picked an isolated spot where there wouldn't likely be tourists. The body had been found in the morning, so the killer must have dumped Theresa before dusk, when the alligators would've been feeding. A smart killer. Patient.

Logan felt the blood drain from his face as he realized what else it probably told Ella. The killer knew specific details about the marsh. "He's a local, isn't he?"

Ella turned, and her deep brown eyes seemed to bore holes through him. "He's not a typical tourist passing through for a week or two. He could be a local, either here or in one of the neighboring towns. At the very least, he's been holed up here for a few months, getting familiar with the town and trolling for victims."

A string of curses burst from deep within, a sour, sick feeling that he might actually know the person who had burned and then murdered his sister's friend.

The sick feeling persisted when his cell phone trilled and the display read Chief Patterson. He hadn't even finished "Hello" before the chief was yelling loudly enough that there was no question Ella could hear every word.

"Why am I hearing about you bringing the *FBI* to Oakville for your ridiculous serial killer theory? How often do you need to hear orders before you follow them, Logan? We're investigating *Theresa's* murder. We are *not* inventing more victims and we are *definitely* not scaring the whole town by turning an isolated crime into a huge spree!"

"Chief—"

"I'm going to tell you this one last time, Logan, and you'd better listen. There's only so far that nepotism can protect your job. You drop this serial killer angle *right now*. Send this profiler home and get back to the station."

"Chief, listen—"

The sudden dial tone cut him off. As he tucked his phone back inside his pocket, he prayed he'd made the right decision in bringing Ella here, prayed that one crazy theory wasn't going to bring down the career he'd fought so hard for.

Chapter Three

"Why isn't she on a plane?" Chief Patterson folded his arms on his desk, glaring with an intensity he seemed to save just for Logan.

Chief Patterson was his father's age. He'd headed up the Oakville PD for twenty years and his dislike of anyone with the last name Greer came from way before Logan's time. Part of it had to do with the Greers' long history of prominent positions in Oakville. And part of it had to do with the chief courting his mother before his father won her away.

Logan looked through the glass door of the chief's office to where Ella sat perched on a chair along the wall, attracting attention from

far too many members of their all-male police
force. Logan scowled. She was here to consult
on *his* case.

"Logan," Chief Patterson snapped, making
his head whip back around. "What part of my
orders was unclear to you?"

"Listen, Chief, Agent Cortez agrees this crime
looks serial."

The chief's scowl deepened, intensifying the
lines that raked across his forehead and bracketed his mouth. "I don't care *what* she thinks. I
don't buy into that profiling hokum. And I am
not going to scare away all our tourism revenue
with some ridiculous theory. If you keep pursuing this angle, I'm taking you off the case. I'll
assign it to someone else."

But Logan knew that none of the other detectives in their small police force would want to
touch the case, not after he'd had his hands on it.
Just like none of them wanted to risk the chief's
ire by partnering with a cop named Greer. The
uniforms joked that the position of his partner

was like a revolving door. Right now, he was the only member of the force without a partner—which was true for most of his tenure as a detective.

But it didn't matter if there was another detective who'd take this case; Logan wasn't handing it over to anyone.

The chief didn't give him a chance to say that, merely held up a hand. "There's nothing your father can do about it. I won't be cowed by political pressure. This is *my* office. I'm your boss and you'd better get used to it."

Logan clamped down hard on his instant response. Not once had he ever used his family's name—or his father's position as mayor of Oakville—to get ahead in his job. If anything, they had held him back.

He fought to keep his voice level. "And this is *my* case. I can't ignore a potential lead because it might hurt tourism."

"Trying to invent a serial killer is *not* a lead," the chief barked. "If you find another body, then it might become a lead, but we don't have any active missing-persons cases, much less any other victims. So, you're *not* spending resources chasing this. Send the profiler home. Get back to work figuring out who had it in for Theresa Crowley."

The chief leaned back in his chair and opened the file in front of him, which meant Logan was being dismissed.

He didn't move. The problem with the chief's plan was that no one had it in for Theresa, or at least no one in the state of Florida. Theresa had spent her entire trip with his sister and their family, so she hadn't had time to meet anyone unsavory. And it was unlikely she'd run into someone she knew on her drive to the airport.

Every investigative instinct in his body was clamoring that Theresa's killer hadn't known her personally, and that if he wasn't stopped, he was going to strike again. To solve the case, he needed Ella. And he owed it to his sister to make sure Theresa's killer was caught.

The chief looked up from his file, raising his eyebrows as he glanced pointedly from Logan to the door.

Instead, Logan took a deep breath and did something he'd sworn he would never do. Something that might well be career suicide.

"Fine. But if you insist I stop working with Agent Cortez and another body *does* turn up, I'm going to the paper to tell them we had a profiler here and you sent her home." He didn't need to add that because of his last name, the story was guaranteed front-page coverage.

A deep red flush spread across the chief's cheeks all the way to his ears, and when he spoke, his voice was an octave too high. "Fine, Logan. You want to play it this way? Then if you're wrong and no other body turns up, but you're too busy chasing an imaginary serial murderer to catch the real killer, I'll be the one talking to the press. And it'll be to tell them why you've handed in your badge."

WHAT WAS SHE THINKING?

Ella stared up at Logan as he held the car door for her to get out and follow him into his parents' house for dinner. When he'd initially told her he had dinner plans with his family, she'd expected to be eating at the hotel's tiny restaurant by herself. But Logan's Southern-boy manners had him inviting her along, and his Southern-boy charm had her stupidly agreeing.

Now that Logan had told his family she was coming and it was too late to change her mind, she wished she'd gone back to the hotel instead. It had been ages since she'd eaten with her own parents and two younger brothers back in Indiana; joining the family of a homicide detective she barely knew was just strange. She wasn't even inside and she was already uncomfortable.

Logan was still standing with his hand on the car door. "You planning to sit in there all evening?"

"And miss the chance to meet this famous

family of yours?" She managed a smile as she climbed out of the car. "Not likely."

"Great," Logan muttered, shutting the door and escorting her to the house.

It was a big white colonial with columns in the front, surrounded by magnolia trees. It looked as if it belonged in the Old South, so Ella wasn't surprised when the door opened to reveal a foyer that resembled a smaller-scale version of something from *Gone with the Wind*.

This was where Logan had grown up? It was a far cry from the blue-collar neighborhood surrounded by wheat fields where she'd spent her childhood. She wondered what path had taken him from this to becoming a homicide detective.

"Logan!"

The woman who opened the door and wrapped Logan in an immediate hug appeared to be in her early sixties. Dark hair streaked with silver was pulled into a twist and when she let Logan go, Ella realized he had his mother's eyes.

"Mom, this is Ella Cortez. She's consulting with me on my case at work. Ella, this is my mom, Diana Greer."

Ella had expected a dainty handshake from the woman in the pressed khakis and green blouse the same shade as her eyes, but what she got was the kind of tight hug usually reserved for long-lost relatives. "Nice to meet you," she choked out.

"Come in, come in." Diana led them through the foyer and a formal living room back to a connected kitchen and family room that looked casual and lived-in.

This was more like the way she might have imagined Logan's childhood home, with the paperbacks stacked on an end table, a big TV on mute against the far wall, and family pictures lining the walls. Ella resisted the urge to take a closer look at Logan as a boy.

"Logan, your father is just finishing up his speech, and then we'll all sit down for dinner.

Ella, would you like something to drink? An iced tea?"

"Sure."

"Logan?"

"No thanks, Mom." Logan sank onto a long couch positioned against the wall.

Diana poured an iced tea, then handed it to Ella. "So, Ella, tell me about yourself. What do you do that you're working with Logan?"

Ella settled into the chair across from Logan, and smiled at his mom. "Well, I'm with the FBI's Behavioral Analysis Unit in Virginia. I can't really talk about the case, but basically, I create profiles of unknown offenders."

"Sounds mysterious." She glanced over at her son. "Logan, before I forget, do you remember Laura Jameson? She just moved back to town and she doesn't know a lot of people her age. I was talking to her mother the other night at a function and I told her you'd love to take Laura out for dinner tomorrow. I've got her number in the other room for you."

Logan let out a long sigh, a hint of red visible despite the scruff on his cheeks. "Mom, you've got to stop doing this."

"What? It's one date."

"I'm in the middle of a case. I don't have time for one date."

Diana sat in the chair across from Logan, a frown creasing her forehead. "Honey, I already told Laura's mom you'd pick her up at seven." Diana turned back to Ella, and asked, "So, Ella, what made you join the FBI?"

If she hadn't still been focused on not staring slack-jawed at Logan and his mother during their exchange, Ella might have tensed up at the question. As it was, she'd barely opened her mouth to answer when Logan cut in.

"You're going to have to call her back, Mom."

"You can't work all the time, Logan. A few hours—"

"Logan!" The woman who walked into the room in jeans and a T-shirt, her dark brown hair plaited, and who shared the green Greer eyes, was clearly Logan's younger sister.

Even though they lived in the same town and presumably saw each other all the time, Logan gave his sister a tight hug, then said, "Becky, this is Ella Cortez."

Ella stood, self-consciously tugging her T-shirt down over the gun holstered on her hip as Becky hugged her just like Logan's mom had done, with the kind of easy familiarity her own family could never hope to match. At least not with her. Not since a single event had changed her life plans and she'd left Indiana to join the Bureau all those years ago.

The pang of loneliness caught her off guard. There'd been a time when she'd expected to stay in Indiana like her brothers. It had been such a tight-knit community where they lived, with her parents, brothers, and grandparents. Growing up, she'd envisioned herself settling down there, too; working at a safe, normal job, getting married, having kids.

But it had been almost a decade since the Fishhook Rapist had made Maggie his very first victim and all those plans had changed. She'd made her choice. If her family hadn't accepted it by now, they never would.

"Did I just hear you getting roped into another date with some lonely woman?" Becky asked Logan as she flopped onto the couch next to him.

Her tone was light. If it hadn't been for the deep shadows under her red-rimmed eyes, Ella might not have known she was grieving.

Logan scowled at her. "Yeah, well, not this time. And don't worry, Becky, Mom will be after you next."

"Ha!" Becky shot back. "Unlike you, big brother, I just say no."

"Logan—" Diana tried again.

"Not this time, Mom."

Becky looked from Ella to Logan to her mom and then laughed. It sounded rough, the laugh of someone who hadn't found anything funny in a while. "So, how come I've never met you before, Ella? It must be pretty serious if Logan's refusing to go out with whoever Mom's set him up with this time."

Heat crawled up Ella's neck at how easy it was to suddenly imagine she was here in a totally different context. How easy it was to imagine having something "pretty serious" with the intense homicide detective.

What was wrong with her? Logan Greer was a colleague and she had to work with him on what might be the most important case of her career. He was off-limits.

"Ella doesn't live here," Diana said, before she'd mustered a reply.

At the same moment, Logan told her, "Ella's not my date. She's consulting from the FBI."

All humor fled Becky's face, leaving behind a strained expression, and Ella saw not Logan's little sister, but a loved one of a victim.

Ella gave herself a mental slap for losing her

focus. She was here for a case and she was completely failing to maintain proper boundaries.

"FBI?" Becky said, her voice wobbly. "Are you here about Theresa?"

Ella tried not to fidget. "Unofficially, yes."

Becky looked from her to Logan and back again. "So, Logan is right? Becky was murdered by a *serial killer*?"

Ella glanced questioningly at Logan. He shared case theories with his family?

"Guess you're not used to small towns," Logan said, answering her unspoken question. "Nothing is secret here."

She definitely *was* used to small towns; she was from one herself—an old farming community that had gotten partially enveloped by the surrounding college-town melting pot but somehow still kept its close-knit feel. But she wasn't used to being a cop in one. "We're checking into that possibility," Ella said, uncomfortable.

Before Becky could ask anything else, Logan's father strode into the room. Besides being the only member of the Greer family with blue eyes, he looked like an older version of Logan. He stopped in front of her and offered his hand. "I'm Andrew Greer. You must be Ella Cortez. Nice to have you join us."

And suddenly, Ella understood all the references she'd heard the police chief shout over the phone about Logan's family. Everything about Andrew, from his perfect posture to his instant smile and handshake, screamed *politician*. "Thank you. You must be Mayor Greer. Am I correct?"

Andrew gave her a wink and let go of her hand. "Until I get Logan here to succeed me." Logan rolled his eyes, but Andrew continued. "I have to say, I wasn't sure what to think about Logan bringing in a profiler, but now I'm a believer. What gave me away, Ella?"

Ella smiled back at him. So, this was where Logan got his charm. "Trick of the trade. If I divulge all my secrets, they'll kick me out of the club."

"Well, we can't have that." Andrew turned to his wife. "Should we eat?"

"Not yet." Becky stood, folding her arms as she stared at Ella. "Don't you want to question me about Theresa?" She sounded wrung out, but the strength underneath reminded Ella of Logan.

Ella shifted from one foot to the other. At the FBI, she was generally at a remove from the investigations. Most of the time, she didn't even leave Virginia—she consulted on a case directly from a police file. When she did travel somewhere to give a criminal personality profile, she still didn't do interviews—except on rare occasions with suspects. She was almost never involved in questioning the friends and families of victims. And she didn't want to start with Logan's little sister.

"Becky, we already took your statement," Logan said quietly, getting to his feet and putting a hand on his sister's shoulder.

"What if Ella has different questions?"

"I usually work from the police files," Ella said gently, forcing herself to look directly into Becky's misery-filled eyes. "If there's something else I need, I'll let your brother know."

"Well—" Andrew started, in his cheery, politician's voice.

Becky cut him off. "Okay. But just answer this for me—how would Theresa have run into a serial killer? It's not like we were out partying with weirdos." Her voice broke, but she composed herself and managed to say, "We hung out at the beach. We went dancing at the club right in town. We went shopping. It was mostly just the two of us. I don't think she talked to a single person I didn't know." She looked from Logan to Ella, tears filling her eyes. Her voice wobbled when she asked, "Did *I* introduce her to the person who killed her?"

"No," Logan insisted. "This isn't your fault."

"There's a good chance that whoever killed her never even spoke to her," Ella said.

Relief broke through the misery in Becky's eyes. "Really?"

"Really."

Becky wiped her hand over her eyes and squared her shoulders. "Okay. Let's go have dinner." She hurried out of the room and after sharing a concerned glance, her parents followed.

Alone in the family room, Logan put his hand on Ella's arm and said softly, "Thank you."

Ella shrugged, trying to ignore how close Logan was standing, how sensitive the skin under his fingers had suddenly become, and trying to distract herself with what she knew. Her job. "There's a very good chance it's true. Yes, the killer had probably been watching Theresa, but it looks like the abduction was an ambush. Someone who does that probably isn't confident. It's unlikely he approached his victims first."

She took a deep breath, aware that she'd been talking too fast, that Logan hadn't taken his hand off her arm. Was it her imagination or had he shifted closer? She could smell his aftershave, something woodsy that made her want to close her eyes and inhale. She tilted her head back a little farther, gazing up into his eyes.

The moss green that had drawn her in from the moment she met him was just a small ring around his pupils now. The desire in his eyes seemed to heat her whole body.

She wasn't sure if she stretched up on her tiptoes or he leaned down, but his lips were inches from hers, his breath on her face. One hand moved from her arm to the back of her head and he slipped his other hand onto her lower back, pulling her closer.

He gave her plenty of time to do the professional thing and back away, but instead she swayed forward and pressed her mouth to his. The stubble on his chin felt abrasive, but his lips were soft as they slowly brushed hers, as though he was determined to memorize every millimeter.

She was the one who insisted on more, who fused her body tightly to his until he slid his tongue between her lips and backed her against the wall. She wove her fingers through his hair and clung tightly to him as his mouth covered hers. Only a loud clink of silverware against china brought her to her senses.

She turned her head away from Logan's and pried her hands off him. Her legs shook and her face burned even hotter as she met his eyes.

He was breathing as heavily as she was. His eyes were hooded, but she could still see passion there, and she got the feeling that if she asked, he'd forget dinner and follow her back to her hotel.

She actually didn't know if she was going to suggest it until she heard herself say instead, "Sorry. That was a mistake."

Logan blinked, shoved his hands in his pockets, and stared at her. Finally, he gave her that sexy, one-sided grin and winked. "Then try to keep your hands off me." He ran a hand over hair she'd mussed, then headed for the dining room. "Let's go to dinner."

Ella followed more slowly, trying to will her pulse back to a normal rate. *Get it together, Cortez.*

She didn't have time to mess around. There was a killer on the loose. And if she was right and it was the same person who'd raped Maggie back in college, he wasn't going to stay in Florida forever. He'd be going somewhere else soon, looking for a new victim to dangle in front of the FBI, and she'd lose her shot at him.

She owed it to Maggie—and Scott and herself—to catch this guy. Especially since, after almost a decade of silence, the Fishhook Rapist had sent Maggie a letter. As a profiler, Ella knew that unexpected contact like that could be a precursor to physical contact. Much as Maggie had tried to play it cool, Ella knew her friend was secretly terrified. And right now,

Ella might have the chance to end Maggie's years of silent, buried fear.

It didn't matter what Logan Greer did to her libido. She was going to have to figure out how to resist him.

Chapter Four

"How did Logan get the FBI to give him a profiler?" Hank O'Connor leaned against the door frame, blocking Ella's entrance to the Oakville police station with his sheer bulk.

Ella busied herself hefting her briefcase, avoiding eye contact, hoping a quick answer would satisfy him. "We like to get involved if we think there's a serial case."

Hank snorted. "Really? I thought there was some big, long process to get a profiler. He find a way to cut to the front of the line?"

The innuendo in Hank's tone made Ella glance up to his dark brown eyes. Yep, definite laughter there. Which was better than true suspicion about whether proper Bureau protocol had been followed, but not by much. Especially considering the way she'd plastered herself to Logan at his parents' house last night.

A flush started climbing Ella's neck, so she put on her flat, all-business tone. "Once I have enough to provide a useful profile, I'll be on to my next case." She looked pointedly at where he leaned against the door. "If you don't mind, I'm expected in the conference room."

Hank rolled his eyes, but got out of her way. As she passed, he muttered, "Guess it's true. Feds have no sense of humor."

Ella didn't slow her stride, just marched straight to the conference room at the back of the station that Logan had booked so they could go over Theresa's case. It had been this or Logan's house and after last night's kiss, she'd immediately picked the station. Now she wondered if she'd made the wrong choice.

If it got back to her boss at BAU that she'd

agreed to give a profile on her own time, her vacation could be permanent.

A lump the size of her gun formed in her throat. She tried to swallow it down, but it stuck. A pact with Maggie and Scott nearly ten years ago had made her apply to the FBI, but the job had become a huge part of her life. She'd weathered her family's disapproval, the FBI Academy's ruthless selection process, and four years of cutting her teeth on gang cases to get into the BAU.

Her goal all along had been to get to this case. She needed to catch Maggie's rapist, and the hook-shaped burn on the back of Theresa's neck told her this could be her chance, but she really didn't want to sabotage her own career to do it.

"Something wrong?" Logan asked.

Ella stumbled, catching herself on the door frame. She'd been so caught up in her thoughts she hadn't realized she'd arrived at the conference room. "N-no, nothing."

She turned her back to him, pouring a cup

of coffee as a cover for calming herself. She'd never crossed the line with a colleague before. Seeing Logan today was awkward and uncomfortable—despite knowing that after two weeks, she'd never see him again.

That thought made the lump in her throat sink to her gut and settle there uncomfortably as if she'd drunk a pot of coffee on an empty stomach.

You've known him for two days, Ella reminded herself. *You can't be this attached to him already.*

But when she turned around, Logan was perched on the edge of the table, his perfectly groomed dark hair begging her to muss it up again, his green eyes studying her with concern, and she knew she was in trouble.

"You sure you're okay?"

"Fine." Ella set her coffee on the table, then pulled a legal pad and a pen out of her briefcase. "Let's get to work."

Logan settled into the chair next to her, a

respectable distance that somehow still felt too intimate.

"You're the expert," he said, his tone normal, as if he hadn't had his tongue in her mouth last night. "Where should we start?"

She fiddled with her pen, then managed to look up at him. "Let's just…" Ella glanced at the door, making sure it was closed, before she continued, "I just want to be clear that what happened yesterday was an anomaly."

"An *anomaly*?" Laughter curved Logan's lips, but it quickly faded, his tone immediately becoming stiff. "You were pretty clear yesterday that it was a mistake. I got it. It won't happen again."

She nodded. "I know this case is important to you. I'm staying. But if it gets out that I'm not supposed to be here…" She stared into those unreadable green eyes. "I could lose my job."

His hand closed over the top of hers, igniting all the sparks she was trying to ignore.

"I'm not going to do anything to put your job in jeopardy."

She pulled her hand away. "Thanks. Okay, let's get to work. Tell me about the car."

"The car?"

"Theresa's rental car. Was it processed?"

"They're still working it, but prints are a bust. The front of the car had been totally wiped down. Nothing there. We found some prints in the trunk, but those were ruled out. One set we've identified as Theresa's and one was my dad's, probably from when he took her luggage out of the trunk."

"Hmm."

Frustration rang in Logan's voice as he said, "My dad was cleared. My whole family was cleared. The coroner narrowed her time of death down to a pretty small window and we were at a town function. Practically the whole town can alibi us."

"That's not what I was thinking. I was thinking it's too bad he wiped down the whole front of the car instead of just one side."

"Because now we don't know if the killer was in the driver's side or the passenger side?"

"Right. Although possibly he was in both. She could have picked him up voluntarily, placing him in the passenger side, and then later, he drove the car to dump it."

"But you don't think so?"

Ella studied the table, considering, then gazed back up at Logan, working it out aloud. "Well, since Theresa wasn't meeting anyone and was headed for the airport when she disappeared, it looks like an ambush. So, either he stalked her beforehand and waited for his opportunity or he picked her at random because he was looking for a victim and she came along at the right time. Either way, why would she pick him up? Given his knowledge of the dumping spot, he's probably been here a while, so it seems unlikely he'd be hitchhiking."

"Theresa wouldn't pick up a hitchhiker."

"Are you sure?"

Logan gave a tired nod, leaning back in his seat. "She roomed with the sister of a homicide detective in college. Trust me, I drilled that kind of thing into Becky. Call me an overprotective brother, but I asked her about Theresa's safety habits. If anything, I think Becky's stories made Theresa overcautious."

"Okay, well—"

"The spare was on the car." Logan swore. "It didn't really occur to me before, but maybe this guy caught up to her when she was changing her tire. Although obviously, she put the spare on, so he didn't grab her then."

"Maybe that was just the way to meet her. He caused her tire to blow, helped her fix it, then grabbed her."

"He caused the flat? How?"

"Maybe a tack board in some deserted stretch of road he knew she'd take to the airport." An ambush. The way Maggie had been ambushed ten years ago.

Ella pushed back familiar anger and kept going. "That's assuming he was stalking her. Can you think of a spot along the route to the airport that would fit?" To her embarrassment, she'd fallen asleep on the drive from the airport near Fort Meyers to Oakville. Logan had needed to wake her when he'd arrived at her hotel.

Logan clenched his fists and Ella understood every ounce of his frustration. His sister's friend was dead and there wasn't a thing he could do to change that. He could only stop it from happening to someone else.

"Well, Theresa was staying with my sister. The fastest route to the airport would be directly through town to the highway. Once you get on the highway, there are some pretty deserted stretches, just marshland on one side and empty land on the other. It doesn't get busier for a good ten or so miles, once you get closer to Naples."

"Maybe we should have some patrol officers

drive it," Ella suggested. "Not the whole route, but the stretch you're talking about. See if they locate any evidence of a blowout, or if we get lucky, maybe something of Theresa's, since none of her personal items have turned up."

Logan sighed, rubbing his temple. "I'll go talk to the chief. Hang on."

While he was gone, Ella unfolded the map she'd grabbed at the airport and studied the distance from Oakville to Cape Coral, Florida. That was where the Fishhook Rapist—who'd started with Maggie in DC almost ten years ago—had assaulted his most recent known victim. It was only forty miles up the coast. The woman had started her first job after college when she'd been grabbed. Like Maggie, she'd been given Rohypnol before she was raped and branded on the back of her neck with the image of a hook.

Then, just like Maggie, just like every other victim over the past ten years, he'd released her on September first and disappeared. Until the next year, when he would reappear somewhere else in the country to do it again.

Ella had always assumed he'd gone to ground between abductions. She'd never considered that he was claiming victims between each September first. But maybe the ones he released were simply his way of getting attention. Maybe the rest he killed and dumped in marshes so their bodies—branded with his signature—were never found.

And maybe he'd finally made his first mistake.

"THAT'S NOT HOW he abducted Theresa," Logan announced when he returned to the conference room, tucking his cell phone in his pocket. Luckily, he'd called Becky before asking his chief to send a bunch of officers to follow a bad lead. He didn't need any more trouble with Chief Patterson.

"What?" Ella quickly folded a map and tucked

it in the briefcase by her feet, drawing his attention to her bare legs.

In deference to the Florida heat, she was wearing a skirt that didn't make it any easier to keep his distance. It figured that the first woman he'd been this attracted to in years lived in another state and was determined to keep things professional while she was here.

She'd acted flustered during dinner last night, and his mom had definitely guessed something was up. Ella's inability to hide her feelings was such an odd contrast with her ability to quickly dissect the personalities of killers that he was tempted to probe the inconsistency. Preferably with more kissing.

A smile pulled on his lips, and he fought to contain it.

Ella's eyes narrowed. "What?"

"I called my sister." Logan rejoined her at the table. "Theresa's tire went flat when they were together, not when she was on her way to the airport. Becky says it blew close to her house the day before Theresa left and the two of them changed it. That's not how the killer grabbed Theresa."

"So, we still don't know how he targeted Theresa or how he grabbed her. Or where. But it still looks like an ambush to me, so he must've gotten her to stop along the way to the airport— maybe to help him if he pretended *he* had a flat tire?"

Logan shrugged, not convinced. "It's possible, but honestly, I don't see Theresa stopping in a deserted area by herself. Calling the cops to tell them someone was stranded seems more likely."

"Well, let's assume he got her to stop somehow. Maybe he blocked the road."

Logan felt his back teeth grind together as he imagined Theresa punching down on the brakes, relieved not to have hit someone, only to be abducted. As he'd done over and over again during the past few days, he tried not to think about what his sister's friend had endured after that.

When he didn't say anything, Ella suggested,

"The other option is that he met Theresa some-time earlier in the week and set up a meeting with her, but from everything we know, that seems unlikely."

"Yeah, I think you're right about the ambush."

"Well, like I told your sister yesterday, an ambush abduction—instead of some kind of charm approach—suggests the killer isn't likely to have talked to Theresa beforehand. Followed her, yes, but not gotten too close." Her words picked up speed, and he could tell she was in her zone now. "He's probably socially awkward, unmarried, a loner."

Logan grabbed his pen, started jotting notes. This was what he'd been waiting for—the pro-filing magic that would help him stop this killer. "Okay. So, I'm not going to find him trolling for victims in the local bar?"

"Probably not. If he is, he's the guy sitting in the corner by himself watching everyone."

"Well, that sounds creepy."

"Which is why I don't think he'd do it. People might remember him. Plus, he'd be uncomfortable."

Logan readied his pen. "Okay, so if I'm not going to find him by hitting the clubs Theresa and Becky went to, then what?"

"You should still retrace their steps. He might be trolling in the same places. And if he's worried about the fact that we have a body—which he probably is—he might try to talk to the cops to find out what they know."

Logan raised an eyebrow. "Really? That doesn't seem very inconspicuous."

"Well, he'd either try to play it casual—act like a concerned citizen who's shocked at the murder and wants to know how we're keeping everyone else safe. Or, if there's reason to talk to him in the course of the investigation—say, he's working at one of the places Theresa went—he might use that opening to try and find out what we know. Your patrol officers should get the name of anyone they talk to about the case."

Logan frowned, but jotted down the suggestion anyway. "That could be a long list. We don't get many murders in Oakville. We're questioning everyone. What else can you tell me about this guy?"

"He's intelligent. He knew to wipe the car down for prints *and* he dropped it in a spot seemingly unconnected to Theresa's abduction. He disposed of the body in a way that meant we almost didn't have one. Plus, he abducted her once everyone here thought she was already home and apparently no one in Arkansas had noticed she wasn't back yet."

"You think that's important?"

"It would be quite a lucky coincidence. And I don't believe in those. So, yes, I think it's important. I think it means he stalked her first. And I think once the thrill wears off, he'll be trolling for his next victim."

Theresa had been stalked. Logan had gone to dinner one evening with Becky and Theresa, and had joined them for ice cream another day.

And all his police training had failed him. He hadn't noticed the man who was watching and would ultimately kill Theresa. And that man was still out there, still a threat.

The guilt gnawed at his insides, making his throat constrict. He looked away from Ella, but it was too late.

Her hand on his wrist was light, but it affected him more than a stack of case files dropped on his head. He sucked in a deep breath. "Sorry."

"I understand. I have a case like this, too."

He whipped his head back, his guilt morphing into frustration. Since Theresa had died, too many people had told him they understood. Too many people had pretended to know how he felt investigating the person who'd killed his sister's friend, in the town where he was supposed to have kept her safe. He was tired, and he was tired of the placating. His words came out rough and angry and staccato before he could rein them in. "You have a case where you didn't protect someone and that person was murdered?"

He knew he'd crossed the line even before her dark brown eyes shifted to near-black, before her jaw jutted out, and she replied, "Well, that's not what I was talking about, but actually, I do."

She didn't give him time to apologize, just grabbed his hand and placed it just underneath the hem of her skirt.

His brain instantly shut down. When it started working again, he realized the skin on her thigh was puckered and rough. A scar.

"I got one bullet to the leg. Just missed my femoral artery or I wouldn't be here. My partner got two bullets, both to the chest. He didn't make it."

She jumped to her feet and turned her back to him, but he heard her shaky, indrawn breath. "I was a newbie in the gangs unit. My partner had been there for years. We got a tip and it went bad. Intellectually, I know there was nothing

I could have done, but that doesn't really stop me from feeling it was at least partly my fault."

She spun back around, and her anger was palpable. "Let's take a break."

She had already left the conference room before he'd finished saying sorry.

Almost instantly, she ran back in. "Logan, get out here."

"What?" He jumped to his feet and followed her.

At the front of the station, through the glass separating the area open to the public from the secure area, he could see a group of cops gathered around someone. Even Chief Patterson was there, his body hunched forward. Logan didn't need to be able to hear what they were saying to read their tone, and it was grim.

He hurried past the station's bullpen out through the key-card doors to the front desk area, with Ella right behind him. They pushed their way around the crowd until they could see the focus of the cops' attention.

It was a woman in her twenties, wearing a T-shirt she'd put on backward and jeans. Her long blond hair fell in a tangled mess. Thin streaks of mascara bled down her face, tears still falling, and even from a distance, the smell of alcohol seeped from her.

"I'm telling you, this isn't like her," the woman cried. "She should have been back at the hotel by now!"

"How long has she been missing, ma'am?" the chief asked. His calm tone didn't match the anxiety radiating from him.

"My name is Kelly. And she went missing yesterday. We were planning to drive home this morning, but we decided to stay a few more days, so we went to the club last night."

"Did your friend leave with anyone, Kelly?" the chief pressed.

"No. Look, I lost track of her at the club, so I went back to the hotel and fell asleep. When I woke up this morning, she still wasn't back."

"Have you tried calling her? Is it possible she went home with someone?"

"Yes, I tried calling her! It goes straight to voice mail. And Laurie's not like that. She likes to party, sure, but she doesn't go home with random guys."

"Do you have a picture?" Ella spoke up.

Kelly turned toward Ella. Maybe because she was the only other woman in the room, Kelly rushed over, digging around in the purse dangling from her shoulder until she pulled out a camera. "Here." She held it out to Ella, an image on the screen.

Logan leaned over Ella's shoulder to see it and an anvil seemed to punch through his chest, leaving behind a deep fear of just what evil Oakville was facing.

The woman in the picture had long, dark hair, just like Theresa. She looked like a college student, just like Theresa. And right before she was supposed to leave town, she'd gone missing. Just like Theresa.

Oakville's serial killer had found his next victim.

Chapter Five

"Let's go over it one more time."

Logan's expression was mild, but even through the one-way glass, Ella could see the strain lurking below the surface. Across from him, Kelly slumped in her seat, her hands trembling around her third cup of coffee. It was hard to tell if the coffee had sobered her up or just made her jittery, along with hungover.

"I've told you everything," Kelly groaned. "Why are we still talking? Go out and find her." Her voice shook when she added, "Look in the marsh where that other girl was found."

Logan leaned closer, his face softening. "We have officers searching for Laurie right now.

I'm asking you to tell me again because some-times the smallest detail—the thing you think is unimportant—is what matters."

He was good at this. Ella had listened to a lot of police interviews in the past two years and she'd learned that the best detectives were pa-tient. Kelly had already told the story twice, but certain little details had been off just enough that Ella knew she was hiding something. Whatever it was, it might be the key to finding Laurie—and maybe to finding their perp.

"So far the marsh is clear."

Ella spun to face the officer who'd come into the observation room as he dragged a chair to-ward the glass and slumped into it.

"What about the bars?" It had been four hours since Kelly had shown up at the station and officers had been sent out to talk to everyone who worked at the bars she and Laurie had hit before Laurie disappeared.

The officer blinked bloodshot eyes, and Ella realized he was one of the second shift officers who'd been called back in to join in the search. "So far, we've got a number of people who remember Laurie. Apparently, she was drinking a lot and being pretty loud. And dancing with half the local boys."

"Does anyone remember her leaving with someone?"

"Not yet. But we have two reports of her mentioning that she was driving home first thing in the morning."

Ella frowned. "Kelly says they changed their mind about leaving this morning, that they were going to stay a few more days."

The officer shrugged. "That's all I know."

"Huh."

"What?"

Ella glanced down at him. "Maybe that's what Kelly's lying about. Maybe they really did plan to leave today."

"Why would she lie about that?"

"I have no idea."

"Why do you think she's lying about anything?"

Ella gestured through the one-way glass to where Logan had gotten Kelly back to the point in her story where she said she'd lost track of Laurie.

Kelly fidgeted, staring down at her coffee cup. "I just turned around and realized she wasn't there anymore. I couldn't find her, so I figured I'd see her back at the hotel."

"And you were on the dance floor when you realized this?"

"Yeah."

Logan didn't say anything for a long moment, and Kelly looked back up at him. "When you talked about this earlier," he said, "you told me you were up at the bar."

Kelly scowled, turning the coffee cup around and around. "Whatever. Why does it matter?"

"You did talk to her before you went back to the hotel, didn't you, Kelly?"

Kelly's shoulders dropped just as the chief

walked into the observation room behind Ella. "Yeah, okay. I was afraid you wouldn't look for her if I told you…"

The chief crowded between Ella and the officer, leaning toward the glass. "I knew there was more to this," he muttered.

"She was talking to a couple of guys, okay? She wanted to stay at the bar longer, but I was tired."

"We need a description of these guys, Kelly," Logan said, only a hint of frustration in his voice.

Kelly waved a hand in front of her. "Okay, yes, she was trying to pick one of them up, but it wasn't going to happen!"

"We still need those descriptions."

"She texted me an hour later. Said the guy had a girlfriend, and she was going to have another drink and then come back."

Ella glanced at the chief, who was standing so close to her she could see the individual strands of silver weaving through his dark blond hair. "I knew it," he mumbled, but he sounded relieved.

The officer straightened in his chair. "Maybe she wasn't grabbed on her way back to the hotel. Maybe she went home with someone."

Ella frowned. "Maybe."

The chief looked at Ella as Logan had Kelly describe the men Laurie had talked to at the bar. "I thought you said the killer was socially awkward?" the chief pressed.

"Well—"

"The profile you gave Logan said he wasn't charming these women, that he wouldn't troll at bars."

"That's true—"

"So, either Laurie went home with someone she picked up at a bar who *isn't* the killer or your profile is wrong. Which one is it?"

"Profiling isn't an exact science," Ella said as the door opened again and Hank O'Connor ran in. "I don't think this killer would be picking up women at bars, but—"

The chief gestured to the interrogation room. "It sure sounds like she didn't leave that bar alone."

"That's true," Hank said. "We've got reports from a couple of tourists at the last bar they hit that Laurie left with another spring breaker. Tall blond kid who was hitting on every girl in the room."

The chief looked pointedly at Ella, his tone mocking. "That sound like your serial killer?"

AFTER SPENDING A long day trying—and failing—to track down Laurie, Ella fell into a deep sleep. If she dreamed of bodies surfacing in marshes and women with burns on their necks, she didn't remember it. She woke to the sound of a door slamming.

"Let's *go!*" a man's voice, full of panic, called.

Ella blinked the sleep from her eyes and threw off the covers. When she peeked into the hotel hallway, she saw a pair of women hurrying toward the front lobby, lugging suitcases behind them. Across the hall, a man pushed open his door, holding it for a woman who was still jamming clothes in a duffel bag as she walked.

"Excuse me," Ella said, "What's going on?"

The man gave her an incredulous look. "You didn't hear? There's a killer in Oakville. Some sicko targeting women on spring break. If you're alone, I'd get out of here now. I'm taking my girlfriend home."

The woman, a tiny brunette in her early twenties, rolled her eyes as she passed her boyfriend. "We're heading up the coast. We're going to find a beach that doesn't have a serial killer feeding people to the alligators."

Apparently the news was out. The locals at least had already known about Theresa, but the serial killer angle hadn't seemed to catch on. Until now.

"Thanks," Ella managed, closing the door to change out of her pajamas and into another skirt and T-shirt that would be sticking to her by midday.

She grabbed her phone, but instead of calling Logan, walked to the hotel lobby. Near the check-in desk was a stack of newspapers. Weaving through the crowd of tanned and hungover spring breakers standing in line to check out early, Ella opened a paper.

The headline for the lead story screamed out, Serial Killer Stalks Coeds in Oakville.

Dropping some change for the paper, she carried it back to her room, reading as she walked. The reporter had led with a quote from Kelly about Laurie's disappearance. After a few paragraphs theorizing on the serial killer angle, he'd shifted into summarizing Theresa's murder—including details of the burns she'd sustained.

Ella cursed as she let herself back into her room. If Theresa's killer had murdered before, he'd managed to destroy all evidence in the marsh. Now, between Theresa's body showing up, Laurie's disappearance and the sudden media flurry, he was either going to go to ground or he was going to forget about being careful and troll for as many victims as he could, as fast as he could.

Which meant she needed to get to the Oakville police station and help them find him before either of those things happened.

She picked up her briefcase and crammed her notes back inside. She was locking the hotel room behind her when her cell phone rang. "Logan," she answered without looking. "I'm on my way."

"Good to know. But this isn't Logan," Scott drawled.

"Scott." Ella forced herself to keep moving. The police station was two blocks over; usually Logan called and picked her up, but today she was glad to have the time to herself. "I'm sorry I haven't called." She tried to put a cheery note in her voice. "How's California?"

"Well, I'd rather you were the one hitting the spa with Maggie, but otherwise, not bad."

Ella couldn't help feeling guilty. Normally when the three of them went on trips together, she and Maggie spent a certain amount of time pampering themselves while Scott took off on his own, usually chasing skirts. "You're not letting her out of your sight, are you?"

"Are you kidding me?" There was nothing funny in Scott's tone. "Maggie may be the SWAT agent, but I'm still her big brother. I'm sticking close."

Not that Maggie should be in any immediate danger, even if Ella was wrong and the Fishhook Rapist wasn't still in Florida. He had never gone back for any of his victims. But they'd planned the vacation a few months ago, when Maggie had gotten a letter, in which the writer claimed to be him.

The letter hadn't made any threats. If the sender hadn't made reference to an evening in September nearly a decade ago, you might have thought it was a love letter. It made Ella feel nauseated just thinking about it.

Follow-up by a case agent had revealed that he hadn't communicated with any of his other victims. The FBI lab hadn't been able to get anything useful off of Maggie's letter. And none of them were really sure how the Fishhook Rapist had tracked down Maggie's address. Follow-up on the postbox in Georgia from which the letter had been sent hadn't given them anything useful. Without any real leads, that had seemed to be the end of it.

But ever since the letter had arrived, she and Scott had made a vow to watch out for Maggie. Between the three of them, Scott and Maggie were the most trained and skilled in a fight. Maggie had been with the Washington Field Office's SWAT team for the past four years and Scott had joined the FBI's Hostage Rescue Team as a sniper a year ago.

Ella knew she could help best by being here, and now that she had just Scott on the phone... She opened her mouth to tell him why she'd bailed on their vacation, but he spoke first.

"Maggie got another letter."

Anger flooded her system, mixed with a

heavy hit of fear. Sudden contact like this wasn't good. Especially if it was escalating. "When?"

"The day we left for California."

Which explained why Maggie had looked so uneasy at the airport. The guilt Ella had been holding back burst like a broken dam. "Where was it postmarked from?"

"Some town in Florida."

"Not Cape Coral?"

"No. Somewhere north of there."

So not Oakville, either. "What did the letter say?"

"Same old crap," Scott said, fury simmering in his voice. "No overt threats, just…his sick fantasy."

"I'm so sorry I'm not there."

She'd spoken so quietly she wasn't even sure Scott had heard her until he replied, "Are you going to tell me why you're not?"

"I got a case—"

"I've known you all your life, kiddo." Beneath the anger over what was happening to Maggie, there was a hint of annoyance in his tone. "Give it to me straight."

"Really. Logan came to me with a case. I was planning to read the file, give him a quick analysis, and get to the airport. But when I read it..." Ella let out a heavy breath. "Scott, I'm in Florida. A place called Oakville, south of Cape Coral. The victim here was murdered and dumped in the marsh, but first she was burned on the back of her neck. Too much decomp to tell for sure, but it could be a hook."

There was a long pause before Scott said, "You took the case on your own."

It wasn't a question, but Ella answered anyway. "Yes. I still don't know if they're connected, but this girl looks a lot like Maggie did ten years ago. And if it is the same person... Scott, I might be able to catch him before another September first comes around."

There was a strong protective note in Scott's voice when he warned her, "Be careful, Ella. And call me. I want updates. Every day, okay?"

"Yeah, okay. You're not going to say anything to Maggie, are you? Not until I know for sure?"

"No, I'll wait. She actually bought your story. And she's relaxed for the first time in months. The beach is doing her good."

"That's great." Ella raised her head and realized she'd reached the police station. She didn't even remember walking there, didn't remember leaving the long dirt trail behind the hotel and arriving in the main part of town, where the station was located. "I've got to go."

"Be careful, Ella. Hurry and get this guy and join us in California, okay?"

"Believe me, I'm trying. I'll talk to you soon."

Hanging up, Ella walked into the station, which was brimming with cops, but not as many as yesterday. One of them let her into the locked back area and she spotted Logan almost immediately, pouring himself a cup of coffee from one of the station's carafes that seemed to be everywhere. His hair was sticking up on top, she could tell even from a distance that there were circles under his eyes, and he was still wearing the jeans and green T-shirt he'd had on the day before.

Ella hurried over to him. "Did you come straight back here after you dropped me off last night?"

Logan looked up with surprise, apparently so tired he hadn't even heard her approach. "I hadn't planned on it, but I got a call that they found the guy Laurie left the bar with."

Ella grabbed his arm, her eyes widening. "And?"

Logan shifted his coffee mug to his other hand. "We still haven't found Laurie. I spent a lot of the night questioning Jeff, the kid who was with her. Local, twenty-one, lived here all his life. He's got a reputation with the women, but nothing violent, no record. He says she went back to his apartment with him, but that she left around three a.m. and he figured she was home by now. He claims he didn't take her number, that she didn't ask for his."

"You could have called me last night. I would have come back."

"No need." Logan rubbed the back of his hand over his eyes, took a long swallow of coffee. "Jeff shares an apartment with a friend, who came home around two, when the bars closed. His friend alibis him, says the girl left and that Jeff was home until we came to question him."

Ella frowned. Her gut told her Laurie's disappearance was connected to Theresa's and that the killer wouldn't have picked her up at a bar. But whenever someone went missing after going someplace alone with a stranger, you had to consider that stranger suspect number one. "You believe the alibi?"

"Yeah. And, honestly, I've met this kid on occasion. He's a surfer and he's got a reputation there, too."

"So?"

"His reputation is that he surfs because he thinks it's a good way to pick up women, but he's a wimp. Apparently he's afraid of just about everything in the ocean. He runs to shore a lot, afraid he's seen a shark fin, only to have his friends make fun of his fear of dolphins. I don't see him going to the marshes when the alligators are feeding."

"Oh." Ella sighed. "So, we've still got nothing?"

"Pretty much. At this point, most of the station believes Laurie is sleeping it off somewhere and that she'll show up soon."

"But not you, right?"

"No. Laurie's picture looked too much like Theresa for me to accept that this is a coincidence."

"About that—" Ella looked around, then realized she still had her hand on Logan's arm. Flushing, she quickly dropped it to her side. "Can we grab the conference room? I want to talk to you about something."

Logan grinned and even with his bloodshot eyes and rumpled, day-old clothes, it shot Ella's heart rate up. "I hope it's about going to dinner at my parents' house again."

His parents' house. Where she'd thrown herself at him. She felt her cheeks color and turned away from him before he could notice, heading for the conference room where they'd worked yesterday. "It's about why I'm really here."

"I WAS WONDERING when you were going to spill your big secret." Logan perched on the edge of the conference table as Ella closed the door behind them.

When she turned to face him, she looked nervous, making him wonder just how bad her news was. "If you're telling me, you must be pretty sure Theresa's murder is connected to the old case you had, right?"

Ella ran a hand through her long hair, pushing it out of her face. "It's not..." She closed her eyes briefly. "It's not exactly an old case, Logan."

He sat a little straighter, praying she wasn't

about to tell him she'd personally known the murder victim she thought was connected to his case.

She let out a heavy sigh, and then, to his surprise, she walked over and lifted herself up onto the table beside him. "When I was in my senior year of college, one of my best friends was abducted."

Sympathy and dread mingled, and a wave of sorrow rushed over him at the thought of Ella having to endure that. "Oh, man, Ella, I'm so sorry."

He didn't even realize he'd threaded his fingers through hers until she looked down at their entwined hands and then back up at him. The expression in her eyes—a mixture of sadness, determination, and something that looked an awful lot like affection—made him want to wrap his arm around her shoulder and haul her close. Instead, he tightened his hold on her hand, trying to tell her without words that there was nothing she couldn't share with him.

Her lips trembled, as though she was trying to smile at him but couldn't manage it, and then she continued, "We shared a dorm room. Honestly, I was worried when she didn't come home that night, but I thought she…" Ella's shoulders jerked and she shook her head. "I knew she and her boyfriend had been talking about taking things to the next level. I thought she was with him and she'd forgotten to tell me."

And she'd probably carried around the guilt of not going to the police sooner ever since. "It's not your fault, Ella."

Her dark brown eyes were more serious than he'd ever seen them as she replied, "Yeah, I know that. But it doesn't mean I'll ever forget how wrong I was."

And when she finished college, she'd picked a job that required her to be right about that kind of predator pretty much one hundred percent of the time. So, apparently, she'd never really forgiven herself, either.

From the few days he'd known her, Ella had

shown a quick wit, an easy smile, so much personable confidence. He'd never for a second have guessed she had tragedy in her past.

"Then, the next morning, when she stumbled back to the room—"

"Whoa. She's alive?" Logan interrupted.

Ella's face twisted. "Yes. It was Maggie. My friend you met at the airport."

The woman with the pretty, but haunted, blue eyes. "What happened to her?"

The emotion left Ella's voice and Logan recognized her clinical, detached profiler mode instantly. "She was raped. And he branded her on the back of her neck with the image of a hook."

A heavy weight sank to the bottom of Logan's stomach. "The Fishhook Rapist?" Every fall, Logan hoped not to see that name in the national news, but each year, it was there again. And this past September, he'd come to Florida. "You think the Fishhook Rapist is now a killer?"

"I think maybe he was always killing in between and we just never knew it."

Logan let out a string of curses. "The burns on Theresa's body," he said. "That's why you asked me if they could've been brands."

"Yes." Ella pulled her hand from his, turning to face him. "Logan, back in college, Maggie had long dark hair. She looked a lot like Theresa."

Logan felt his shoulders slump. Could this get any worse?

"Logan—"

From Ella's tone, Logan knew it was about to. "What?"

"The Fishhook Rapist seems to pick girls in their late teens or early twenties, girls with long dark hair and slender builds."

"Like Theresa," Logan agreed. "It makes sense. The women he lets go are his way of bragging, and in between, the others feed his twisted need for violence."

"Logan, what I was going to say is that there's someone else who fits that description."

The room seemed to close in around Logan. He felt Ella grab his arm as he realized. "My sister."

Chapter Six

"How sure are you that Theresa's killer is the Fishhook Rapist?" Logan paced back and forth in front of her, running his hands through already messy hair, which made Ella's fingers itch to slide through it, too.

"I'm *not* sure. It's a theory. Based primarily on the hook-shaped burn on Theresa's neck. It looks a heck of a lot like the Fishhook Rapist's signature. But if it is the same person, then we're not looking at a killer who's been getting away with this for a few weeks or months. We're talking about a perpetrator who has eluded the FBI for a decade."

Logan stopped pacing. "Well, that's a cheery thought."

Ella hopped off the table and found herself standing closer to Logan than she'd expected. Close enough to see the scruff on his chin, the sexy curve of his lips. Close enough to imagine how easy it would be to reach her hand up and around the back of his neck, then pull him close and fuse her mouth to his.

Focus, Cortez.

She scooted quickly sideways to create a little distance. He inhaled sharply, as if he knew what she'd been thinking.

"Well, if it is the same person, do you think he's sticking around here? The rapes happen once a year, in a different part of the country each time. Is he picking one location in between and killing? Or is he traveling the whole time like those highway serial killers the FBI is always after?"

Ella shrugged, frustrated. "I don't know, Logan. I've studied the Fishhook Rapist for years and I never even considered that he might be killing in between until you brought me your case. But my gut tells me that if it is him, he's not in our HSK database." Because of the number of killers who picked up transient victims, often along highways, the FBI had created a database specifically to track those murders.

"The Fishhook Rapist is a planner in every single detail. And the evidence here suggests careful planning, too. Remember how we talked about his choice of drop site?"

"Knowing the kind of details about the marsh that a local would," Logan agreed.

"Right. So, whether or not this is the same person, I think he's been here a while, planning the details of the murder. And I don't think he intended to leave anytime soon. But with the recent media coverage..." She sank into a conference chair.

"So, what do I tell my sister? Leave town? Stay here and move in with my parents?"

"Honestly, she's probably safer here, with you

looking out for her. But moving in with your parents until we catch this guy is a good idea. Also not going anywhere alone, since this guy is probably ambushing his victims. He most likely stalked Theresa before he killed her. And if Theresa was with Becky the whole time she was here…"

Logan cursed. "Great. Because I wasn't feeling paranoid enough already."

He grabbed the chair next to her, dragging it close so their knees were almost touching. His eyes locked on hers as if she had all the answers. "What else do I tell her to keep her safe, Ella?"

Panic fluttered in Ella's chest. It was part of her job not just to advise on the behavioral makeup of killers, but also how to catch them, and how to keep the population safe until that happened. But the pressure of trying to keep Logan's little sister out of harm—especially if she'd already been targeted—felt too intense, too personal. It felt way too much like her desire to protect Maggie.

A queasy, nervous feeling swam around in her stomach. She'd only known Logan a few days. Of course she wanted to keep his sister safe, but it couldn't be as personal as Maggie. She couldn't let it. Because as soon as she helped Logan catch this killer, she had to leave town. And she'd never see Logan again.

That thought made the queasiness dart upward, tension clamping her chest. She liked this guy, genuinely liked him, way too much.

Even if he didn't live in a different state, her relationships were destined to be short-term. It didn't matter how good her intentions were, how nice the guy was, it always ended after a few months. She'd get one important case after the next, get tunnel-visioned until it ended and then discover the guy hadn't waited around.

"Ella?" Logan was still staring at her, but his gaze had turned questioning. "You okay?"

Ignoring the question, Ella said, "The best

way to keep Becky safe is to keep her close. Drill it into her not to go anywhere she could find herself alone. This guy is smart, but he isn't charming or confident. He's socially awkward. He's not going to approach her in a group somewhere and try to lure her away with him. He's not going to come after her in your parents' house, either. That's not his style. He'd want her to come to him. He'd be waiting for an opportunity to create an ambush and he'd do it somewhere deserted. Just don't give him that chance."

Logan's big hands wrapped around hers, instantly warming them, and sending a suspicious warmth upward. "Thank you, Ella."

Oh, this was not good.

He stood, pulling his phone from his pocket. "I'm going to give her a call." He started pacing as he talked to Becky, gesturing with his free hand as he went into full-on big brother mode.

Ella tracked him with her eyes as he walked, thinking about all the details she had somehow catalogued without realizing it over the past few days. The way his green eyes darkened when he was worried. The way he looked at her with such compassion when he knew she was hurting. The way he could shift from serious, competent homicide detective to easygoing, teasing colleague to intense, irresistible potential lover in a heartbeat.

Oh, she was in so much trouble.

"How come you don't have a partner?"

Logan glanced at Ella as they sped out of town in his Chevy Caprice, grinning as he purposely misunderstood her. "Interested in my love life, are you?"

She flushed and fidgeted and he tried not to laugh. "I meant, why don't you have a partner in your job?"

His smile faded. "Because my last name is Greer."

"Really? Your chief dislikes your dad so much

that he wouldn't assign you a partner? That seems…dangerous."

"Not exactly," Logan said, weaving around traffic as he headed toward the highway that Theresa would have taken to the airport, a stretch of road that was often deserted at night. Where Theresa might have been abducted by a serial killer as she drove to the airport at four in the morning. "But the whole force knows how much the chief resents me, so no one wants any of that coming down on them."

Ella was silent, but one glance at her pensive expression and he knew more questions were coming.

She didn't disappoint. "If it's that bad, there must be easier places to work as a homicide detective. I don't think you'd have trouble getting hired."

"I think you'd better wait until this case is closed before you make predictions like that."

"Oh, come on. You're good at your job. I knew

that the second you showed up at Aquia look-ing for a profiler."

"And yet, you pulled your gun on me," he teased, pleased that she thought he was good at what he did. Getting serious, he added, "I may not be planning to run for mayor or the chief of police like my family wants, but I can't really imagine living anywhere else."

She was silent a little too long, but when he glanced over at her again, she said quickly, "It's nice that you're so close to your family."

"Aren't you?"

"No."

"Really?" How could anyone not be close to Ella? With her determination to help her friend, no matter how it impacted her long-awaited va-cation? With her humor and warmth, despite the grisly things she saw in her job every day? With that quick smile that instantly lit her whole face, made her dark eyes sparkle? Man, she was...perfect.

The steering wheel jerked in his hand, and

he corrected fast, but not before Ella shot him a quizzical look.

She wasn't perfect, he told himself. She only seemed that way because he hadn't had enough time to learn her flaws.

"Yes, really," she said. "They don't approve of my job."

"Why? Because they think it's too dangerous?" Logan slowed as they reached the outskirts of Oakville and turned slowly onto the highway. Cars honked and sped around him, since traffic was much heavier in the daytime. But at night, if a predator knew how to set an ambush, it was the ideal spot.

He and Ella were looking for any sign that Theresa had been forced to stop the car unexpectedly, like skid marks.

"I'm the black sheep," Ella said, as she peered carefully out the car windows, checking both sides of the road. "I was going to stay in Indiana and be a teacher like my dad until Maggie was raped. Then, Scott, Maggie, and I—we'd been best friends since we were little—the three of us made a pact. We were going to join the FBI and stop guys like that from hurting anyone else."

Logan slowed even more as he divided his attention between watching for skid marks and concentrating on what made Ella tick. "And your parents didn't understand that?"

"They wanted me to stay close to home. They figured the FBI thing was just a phase. That's what they call it—my 'FBI thing.' They figured I'd get over it and come back home. Live close to them like my younger brothers. Give them more grandkids and come over every weekend for dinner."

Her shoulders jerked up, as if she was shrugging, as if it didn't matter, but even though she was facing away from him, he could tell it bothered her.

"My parents are from Puerto Rico," she explained. "My dad's second generation, my mom's first. My dad's a professor. He got a job at a university in Indiana and we moved there when I was six. My dad's parents came with us, that's how close we all are. It's like a family motto—don't make big decisions without everyone's input, and stick together. They just don't get how I could leave, especially for a job like this. They moved to this little farming town close to the university, instead of the city where my dad works, because they wanted to live in the kind of small community where everyone knows each other."

Logan imagined how hard it had been for her to tell them she was leaving.

"I went through the long application process, studied and trained like crazy to make it through the eighteen weeks at the Academy. I've been in the Bureau for six years now and still, the first thing I hear when I visit is, 'When are you going to give up that FBI thing and come home?'" She blew out a heavy breath and turned to face him. "So, I visit less and less often."

He started to tell her he was sorry, but she

gave him a stiff smile and said, "But Maggie and Scott live close and they're basically family, too. So, it's not like I'm all alone in the world." The smile shifted into something more real. "So, don't give me that sad look."

"Believe me, there's nothing sad about you." He frowned as the lights ahead grew brighter and he still saw no sign of foul play. As much as he didn't like picturing someone forcing Theresa to slam her car to a stop, then grabbing her, they needed a lead. And Ella thought identifying how and where she'd been abducted would tell them a lot, help them find the killer. This had seemed the most likely option.

Ella looked discouraged, too. "Maybe he took her at the airport and then just drove out of there with her in the trunk? Some of those long-term lots get pretty empty at night. He could have left in her car and then come back for his own later."

Her tone told him she didn't believe it. "But you don't think so?"

"Not really. It is possible, because I just don't

have enough information about what happened to Theresa to form a truly solid profile of her killer. But that's what's bothering me. It's not an accident that I don't have what I need. This guy is smart. He didn't get close enough to make Theresa or Becky suspicious, he dropped Theresa in a place where her body would disappear. And he grabbed her when no one would notice she was missing until a day later. The airport parking lot seems too uncertain. If someone else was there, then he'd lose his chance and she'd be gone."

"I've been thinking about the timing, too," Logan said. "If he was stalking her, then he knew she was leaving that day. He knew we'd all assume she was home. Maybe he'd looked into her life and knew she lived alone and wouldn't be immediately missed by someone waiting for her to come home from the airport either?"

Ella continued to scan the road, but her tone was grim when she said, "The timing is suspicious. Especially if he has Laurie right now. I know Kelly said they'd changed their minds and planned to stay a few more days, but if they'd originally planned to leave yesterday..."

"It's the same MO," Logan agreed.

There were officers looking for Laurie now, still trying to track her down, and Logan had wanted to spend the rest of his day on that, too. But Ella had convinced him that if questioning witnesses was going to lead them to Laurie, it would happen with or without him. But no one else was following leads on the serial killer angle, because although the media had jumped on the story, the rest of the police force still didn't believe it.

So, instead of heading into town to question anyone who might have seen Laurie, he was searching the highway. But as the scenery turned from barren, closed-down factories on one side and marshland on the other to city lights, he knew there was nothing to find. If Theresa had been taken while she was on the highway, she'd stopped willingly. And he just didn't believe she'd do that for a stranger.

He pulled off to the side, then did a U-turn and headed back toward Oakville. "What do we do now?"

Ella shook her head, looking troubled. "I don't know."

ELLA'S SHOULDER BLADES TENSED, and her steps slowed as she walked along the long, solitary trail toward the back of the hotel. She strained to listen, and there it was again. The sound of a vehicle, its tires rolling slowly along the dirt road somewhere behind her. She hadn't imagined it.

She whipped her head around, but she couldn't see anything in the dim light. The sun was barely peeking over the horizon. The path behind her curved around a dense patch of trees, sending the road out of her line of sight. She could hear the car still coming, slowly. Too slowly, as if it didn't want to be seen.

She should have let Logan drive her back to the hotel. Instead, after a long, frustrating day that had gotten them no closer to finding Laurie or figuring out how Theresa had been grabbed, she'd told him to go get some badly needed sleep. She'd wanted the chance to stretch her legs, walk off some of the tension that had been building inside her with every day that passed without getting any closer to knowing if this case was connected to Maggie's.

During the day, the trail from the hotel was packed with tourists walking into town. Even at night, she'd seen enough people walking it that it hadn't occurred to her it might be empty tonight. But it was late. Apparently late enough that everyone was either out at the bars or back at the hotel.

Ella picked up her pace, resting her palm along the butt of the gun she always wore holstered at her hip. Her pulse jumped as she looked over her shoulder and finally spotted the vehicle, which was rolling along at a walker's pace, clearly trying not to be heard. It was a van, dark blue, and as she squinted, trying to see inside the vehicle, it slowed, easing slightly into the shadows of the trees.

Ella cursed and unholstered her gun. If this guy was planning to run her over, she'd have to shoot accurately and fast. And the only reason anyone in Oakville would be after her was Theresa's case.

She tightened her grip on her weapon, aiming straight at the front windshield.

The van's window rolled down and she darted off the trail where it would be harder for the driver to see or shoot her.

But he just called out, "This isn't the way to Seaside Resort, is it?"

Ella still couldn't really see him, so she kept her weapon raised, but her heart rate evened out. "No, this is the Traveler's Hotel."

"Thanks," he called, obviously unable to tell in the dark that she had a gun. Then he rolled up the window and backed his van down the road and around the corner.

Lowering her weapon, Ella let out a brief burst of laughter. She'd been chasing killers so long she was seeing them everywhere. She definitely needed to finish up this case and go lie on the beach for a week.

Holstering her Glock, Ella walked faster, just a little too relieved once she'd locked herself into her hotel room. Flipping on the television, she changed into her pajamas and flopped onto the bed, ready for an evening of mindless sitcoms.

Before she could find one, there was a heavy knock at the door. Putting the TV on mute, Ella grabbed her Glock and stood off to the side of the door, peeking through the peephole.

"Logan," she breathed, setting her gun on the table by the door. The fact that she'd automatically assumed it was the guy from the blue van, holding a shotgun, confirmed that she needed a break from rummaging around in the minds of demented killers.

Ella opened the door to find Logan staring at his shoes. "I thought you were going home?"

"Ella, I'm sorry. A reporter—" He looked up and stopped midsentence, blinking at her attire.

Suddenly way too conscious of the fact that she was standing in the doorway in a pair of boxer shorts and a tank top with no bra, Ella crossed her arms over her chest. "A reporter what?"

His gaze travelled slowly down to her bare feet and back up again and Ella felt her pulse quicken at the inspection.

Finally he looked into her eyes, and the intensity there seemed to push her backward until he was standing inside her room, the door shut behind him. Then he leaned against it, just watching her.

There was a foot between them, but Ella imagined she could feel his body heat wafting toward her. Her mouth suddenly went dry.

Then Logan took a step forward and the foot became an inch. If she took a deep breath, they'd be touching.

Ella tilted her head back, expecting his mouth to come down on hers, wanting it to. But instead, he raised his hand, cupping her cheek. Then he lowered his head slowly, so slowly, until his lips brushed hers.

The first gentle contact sent sparks of desire from her mouth to her fingertips and Ella pushed up on her tiptoes, gripped the front of his shirt with both hands, and leaned into the kiss. Then Logan opened his mouth and gave her exactly what she wanted.

With a low moan, she tugged him backward until her legs hit the bed and they fell onto it, his body covering hers. She jerked as the TV blasted on, then realized she'd landed on the remote.

Ignoring it, she slid her hands down to his waist, then up under the hem of his T-shirt, over the bunching muscles in his back, as his lips found hers again. One-night stands had never been her style, but she was completely lost as his tongue tangled around hers and his fingers dug into her hips.

"…an FBI profiler in Oakville."

"What?" Ella mumbled against Logan's mouth, trying to sit up as the words from the television penetrated her desire-fogged brain.

Logan glanced behind him at the TV, then let out a string of curses and pushed to his feet.

Instantly cold without his body covering hers, Ella shivered and stood, hugging herself. The TV screen cut to an image of a tall, blonde reporter thrusting a microphone toward Logan outside the police station as he walked out the door. "Detective, you suspect a serial killer is in Oakville?"

Logan looked blindsided as he ducked past the reporter with a "No comment." But there was something more in the deep red that rushed up his cheeks as he hurried toward his Chevy Caprice.

Ella looked questioningly at Logan.

"Ella, I—"

On the TV, the reporter yelled after him, "Is it true the FBI sent a profiler to consult on the case?"

Logan didn't answer, but the damage was done.

Ella sank onto the bed. Her secret was out. And if it got back to her boss in Aquia, there went her job.

Chapter Seven

"Theresa's credit card information just came in." Logan waved the pages at Ella as she entered the conference room where he'd just started working.

He'd been listening for his phone all morning, waiting for her to call and have him pick her up, but the call had never come. She'd walked to the station again. Probably because of what had almost happened between them last night.

As he watched her now, she turned away from him to get a cup of coffee from the carafe on the table. He felt amused by how poorly she hid her emotions. For some reason, as a profiler, he'd expected her to be expressionless most of the time. But Ella's feelings were usually stamped across her face.

Any second now she'd turn back and tell him the same thing she had the first time they'd kissed. That it was an *anomaly*. Which was not only stupid, but he definitely hoped it would be as untrue this time as it had been then.

To his surprise, when she squared her shoulders and turned around, she said, "If my boss gets wind of the fact that I'm here without permission, he's going to call me back to Aquia."

She rubbed the back of her neck and he suddenly noticed the deep circles under her eyes. She'd been up worrying about this, he realized. He wished she'd let him stick around and distract her instead.

The thought sent a powerful flash of desire through him. It made full-color images of Ella in her little pajama shorts and tank top blast into his brain. Fantasies of her pulling him down on top of her like she had last night. But then he pictured them continuing instead of being interrupted. He pictured her legs wrapping around his waist, her hands in his hair. Her voice, husky with passion, whispering his name.

Logan sucked in a deep breath and tried to blink the images away. He stepped closer, forcing her to look up at him.

"I'm so sorry, Ella. I swear, I tried to keep any knowledge about your presence totally in-station. I don't know how Lyla got hold of it."

"I know you did." She sighed, then squinted at him. "Lyla?"

Logan felt his face heat. "The reporter at the station."

Her eyes narrowed, filled with suspicion. Served him right for trying to get anything past a profiler.

She opened her mouth, so he preempted her, "Yes, we used to go out."

Something flashed in Ella's eyes. "It was pretty serious, I take it?"

When he didn't immediately answer, she

cringed a little and he realized what he'd seen in her eyes. Jealousy.

A smile tugged at his lips, but faded fast as he admitted, "We were engaged."

"Oh." Surprise darted across her features. "Well, that *is* serious."

Before he could tell her it was long over, she hurried on, "Not that it's any of my business. Anyway, I just—I don't know what I'm going to do if my boss calls me back in." She set her coffee down untouched, rolled her shoulders. "I joined the Bureau because of that pact I told you about, the one that Maggie, Scott, and I made. But the job has become more than that. It's become really important to me. It's become…." She trailed off, looking lost and completely torn.

"I understand. If your boss calls, you'd have to leave." He reached out and folded her hand in his as dread and sadness coursed through him in equal measure. He didn't want her to leave. And it was about a heck of a lot more than this case.

She looked down at their entwined hands and tightened her grip. She had small hands, but man, was she strong. It was another one of those incongruities he loved about her.

His hand jerked in hers as he realized what he'd just thought. He felt her curious expression just as he felt himself go a little light-headed. He *did* love her odd little inconsistencies. And that nervous feeling rolling around in the pit of his stomach at the thought of her leaving wasn't simply about the way she looked in that skirt or the way her mouth felt against his.

It was about how she'd gone instantly still and serious when he'd asked her to help him keep his sister safe. It was about how she'd stood up for him in the diner that first day he'd met her. It was about how she made him feel every time he looked at her. Which, even in the middle of a homicide investigation, was freaking *giddy*.

A curse wanted to break out, but he held it in. He didn't believe in love at first sight. And given the short time they'd known each other, that was what it might as well be. Which was completely ridiculous.

This was a complication he hadn't expected. And one he didn't need in the middle of Theresa's case. With a woman who lived too far away, who'd be gone as soon as the case was closed. Or sooner.

"Logan?" Ella's voice sounded remote as she asked, "Are you okay?"

"Not really."

"Look, I know you need my help." She gave a quick nod, as if she'd just made a decision. "I'll work it out. I've got important reasons to stay myself."

He took a deep breath, getting it together, then smiled at her, wishing one of those reasons was him. "Whatever I can do, let me know. I'll talk to your boss if you want."

"Well, thanks, but that's probably not the best idea. I'd rather he didn't find out you put in a request for a profiler that he denied and that

I took the case anyway. I'll figure it out if he calls. Until then, let's see what you've got."

It took him a second to realize she was talking about the credit card information. "Right. Okay." He glanced out the conference room door into the station to make sure no one was within sight. Then, he lifted her hand and pressed it to his lips before letting go.

He saw her surprise as he picked up the thin stack of charge information. "These were faxed in from her credit card companies. I was about to get started on them when you arrived."

She settled into a conference chair and yanked her hair back into a ponytail, her serious face on. "Great. I'll take half."

She held out her hand and he gave her the coffee cup she'd set down beside the carafe, then sat next to her. He slid the charges from half of Theresa's cards over to her, keeping the rest for himself. "I figured I'd start from the end of each statement and work my way backward, see if I found anything interesting."

"Makes sense," Ella said, taking a quick sip of coffee, then flipping to the last page in her pile. "Uh, Logan..."

"What?"

"What time did Theresa leave for the airport?"

He gave her a half smile. "Show-off. You already have something?"

"This past Sunday, at seven a.m., she's got a charge at a gas station."

"Seven?" Logan leaned forward, until Ella's bangs brushed his forehead, as he squinted down at the small text. "Her flight left at six thirty. I checked right after we found her body, confirming that she hadn't changed the flight for some reason, and she hadn't. Obviously, she didn't make it, but because time of death wasn't pinpointed that closely, I assumed someone had already grabbed her by then."

He looked up and found Ella's eyes inches from his. The other times he'd been this close to her, his eyes had been closed as he'd sought out her mouth. Now, he realized her deep brown eyes were the shade of really good dark coffee. He'd expected flecks of lighter brown around the edges, or a hint of some other color up close, but they were just pure, deep brown. They were mesmerizing, and he realized he was staring, but he couldn't seem to stop.

Her pupils dilated and he leaned even closer, reached his hand up to touch her face.

"Logan," Ella said, her voice unsteady. She moved away from him, breaking the spell.

"I'll bet the killer *did* grab her before she could make her flight. This charge probably means Theresa wasn't using the card. I think it was her killer."

"WHAT TIME DID you need again?" the kid at the gas station asked Logan.

Despite looking as if he was still in high school, the pimply-faced kid was the manager on duty. He was sitting in front of a dinosaur-age TV in the back room, rewinding through hours of security footage from last Sunday, which, thank goodness, the gas station hadn't taped over yet.

He also had the attention span of a gnat. He kept glancing over at Ella, who stood beside the kid's chair, hands planted on her hips. The kid couldn't stop staring at her gun. And her legs, which Logan had to admit looked pretty fantastic in the knee-length skirt she wore.

The kid checked out her legs again, and Logan was ready to slap him upside the head. "Ten minutes before seven," he bit out.

"Okay." The kid nodded, still rewinding, and glanced over at Ella again, his eyes practically bugging out of his head. "So, what kind of gun do you carry?"

"One issued by the Federal Bureau of Investigation," she replied dryly, then, "Stop!" as the time stamp on the bottom of the tape reached 6:50 a.m..

On either side of him, she and Logan leaned toward the screen. The kid backed up his chair a little, seeming uncomfortable with their sudden intensity.

On the tiny TV, cars came and went as Logan carefully watched the time stamp. The person who paid at 7:01 a.m. was the one they wanted. That was the guy who had Theresa's credit card. And if he had her card, he was almost certainly the person who'd killed her.

With luck, he'd glance up at the camera, give them a good shot to plaster across every news network. Make it easy to track him down so Logan could slap a pair of cuffs on him.

Maybe the guy would even resist, and Logan would have to use a little force to put him down. The idea made his hands tense hopefully into fists.

Another car pulled out of the gas station, and then a little red compact drew up to a pump. Logan leaned even closer, his jaw locking as the driver's side door opened. And then the driver did look up, right at the camera.

Beside him, Ella did a double take. "Logan, is that…"

His shock was followed by a rush of unease. This wasn't right. This wasn't right at all. Had their investigation been going in completely the wrong direction?

He turned to Ella, and the shock he felt was written all over her face, too. "It's Theresa."

Ella looked at the screen, then at him. Between them, the kid's head swiveled back and forth; a moment later, he ducked his head and pushed his chair backward so he was entirely out of their way.

Logan gestured to the door. "We'll call if we need you."

The kid gave Ella one last longing look, then left them alone.

"Are you sure her flight was at six thirty?" Ella asked.

"Positive."

"So, what's she doing on the opposite side of town half an hour after her flight left?" Ella frowned at the screen, where Theresa held out her key fob, as though she was locking the car doors, then headed inside the building, presumably to pay. "She certainly doesn't look like she's being coerced. It doesn't look like anyone else is in the car, either. I'd thought…"

Ella had thought by 7:00 a.m., Theresa had already been snatched by the killer. That she was already being tortured, that very soon afterward, she would be dead. So had Logan.

"What's she doing here?" Logan mumbled. On the screen, Theresa filled her tank, then got in her car and drove away.

Ella shook her head. "Everything we've been assuming is wrong," she said, glancing quickly at the TV. "This means— Whoa!"

"What?"

"Rewind it!" She scooped up the remote herself.

"What did you see?"

"Hang on." Ella leaned close to the screen as she rewound, then paused. "There!" She pointed to the very edge of the shot, at the front of a blue van that backed out shortly after Theresa's car pulled away.

"What? You think the person in the van is following her? It could be any of the cars here, couldn't it? Or, who knows, she could've been meeting someone after all. I mean, why was she still in town after her flight left?"

"No, Logan." The look on Ella's face was dead serious and slightly apprehensive. "A blue van was following me yesterday."

"What?" Logan grabbed her arm, worry filling him. "When?"

"Last night. Right before you showed up at my hotel. I was walking that trail to the hotel. It was deserted. When the van came up, I actually pulled my gun. But then the guy said something about being confused about directions and took off. I figured I was just getting paranoid."

She let out a string of curses so creative Logan felt his eyebrows rise; they would've made him laugh had this not been so serious. "You think Theresa's killer was following you?"

Ella glanced down at his hand on her arm, and he realized he was squeezing.

He relaxed his hold, trying at the same time to loosen the grip panic had on him. Ella was a trained FBI agent who carried a weapon. And, judging by the surprising strength he'd felt in her arms, she could hold her own in a fight.

"I don't know. I can't actually be sure he was following me. Plus, it was dark. It was a guy in the van, that I know from his voice, but I couldn't see him. And how common are blue vans?" She sighed. "But we'd better check this out, because it seems too coincidental that a blue van shows up on the last image we have of Theresa before she died—and there was one at my hotel last night."

She pulled her arm free from his grip. "We'd better get Theresa's phone records, too, and see if she called someone that day. See if we can figure out why she wasn't on that flight."

"I've been working on that. It's a process. Warrants and all. But they should be on their way now."

Ella looked troubled as she turned to him again, and this time it had nothing to do with her fear of who'd been following her the other night. "Logan, we should push the phone company and get them to do it faster. If she *was* meeting someone that day, we might be going at this all wrong. Maybe she called some old boyfriend who lived around here. Or he called her, convinced her to come see him and catch a later flight. This could be a single murder with a typical motive."

She hustled to the door, opened it and called out to the kid, "We need a copy of this tape."

The kid rushed back in to do her bidding and as Ella sank into a chair to wait, Logan heard her mumble, "Maybe this isn't a serial killer at all."

Chapter Eight

Logan's ex-fiancée was tall, thin and blonde. She had the kind of face that made her an obvious choice for an on-camera reporter and the kind of body that could have modeled underwear. She was absurdly perfect-looking, like a supermodel who'd stepped out of the pages of a magazine, still air-brushed.

Ella would have been happy to go her entire life without knowing that was Logan's type.

When Logan had told her this morning that the reporter she'd seen on the TV last night was his fiancée, she'd tried not to react. And she'd tried not to think about it all afternoon as they ran down leads.

Now she stood in the police station bathroom, staring at herself in the mirror above the sink. Compared to Lyla's blonde perfection, Ella was ordinary—with plain brown eyes and plain brown hair. She was average height, with ropey muscle hiding underneath her curves, a mouth just a little too big for her face and bags under her eyes after a sleepless night.

Get a grip, Cortez.

It didn't matter what Logan's type was, because she wasn't going to stick around long enough for it to matter. And if that thought made her chest feel a little too tight, she was just going to have to deal with it.

She was here to catch a killer. And she needed to get back to it.

Straightening her spine, she pushed open the door and found Logan waiting for her.

"Did you get Theresa's phone records yet?" she asked.

"The phone company is faxing them over right now. They should be here soon," Logan said, walking with her toward the conference room they'd staked out earlier in the day. "I just went to the vending machines while you were in the bathroom." He held out a candy bar. "Thought you might want something to hold you over until we grab some real food," he said, peeling back the wrapper on his own candy.

"Thanks." Ella took a big bite, savoring the chocolate, then said, "I know this isn't what you want to hear, but I think you'd better talk to your sister again, Logan."

"I know. I've also got some officers tracking down the license plates from the other cars that were at the gas station, in case any of those people saw Theresa."

"The tech couldn't get a license on the blue van, could he?"

Logan shook his head. "The van never pulled far enough into the station to get a shot of the plate. It was parked right by the pump for air, but if the driver ever got out to fill his tires, he's out of the frame, too." Logan shrugged.

"The air is free, so the gas station wasn't worried about having that area covered by the cameras. The guy could very well have been there legitimately. We just can't tell."

Ella put her hand on Logan's arm, stopping him as they reached the conference room. "But someone's running down a list of locals who own blue vans, right?" Just like anyone else, she occasionally got spooked by nothing, but she wasn't the type to pull her gun at every imagined threat. She sensed that she needed to follow up.

"I'm checking on those myself, Ella, in Oakville and the surrounding towns. In the meantime, maybe we should move you to a different hotel."

She smiled. "I'm armed. And the Bureau believes pretty strongly in teaching its agents defensive training. Believe me, I got the bruises to prove it back at the Academy, but I learned. This guy doesn't want to mess with me."

Logan didn't look any less worried. "I'd still

feel better if you were somewhere else. You can stay with me if you want. I have an extra bedroom."

Her nerve endings tingled at the idea, but Ella forced herself to give him a look of disbelief. "Yeah, because that would really work." If she stayed at his house, she'd end up in his bed, and they both knew it. Appealing as it might sound, that idea had *heartbreak* written all over it. And she didn't have time to mess around.

"I'm fine where I am. If it's the same person, he's not coming after me in a busy hotel. And I'm not using that shortcut to the station anymore. I'm taking the long way around."

Ella moved to go into the conference room, but Logan stepped in front of her, blocking her way, close enough to make her tip her head back to look at him. "That idea may have held when we were talking about a killer who ambushed his victims in deserted areas, but not anymore, Ella."

"Logan—"

"Humor me, okay? Please."

Deep furrows appeared in Logan's forehead, and Ella realized he was dead serious. He was really afraid Theresa's killer was targeting her, too. He was truly, deeply worried about her.

A rush of warmth went through her as she tried not to smile.

Although the idea of someone tracking her did have her concerned, the truth was, she could take care of herself. And even if she was wrong about how the killer was abducting his victims, she wasn't wrong about his intelligence or his desire to keep a low profile. Since the media flurry hadn't sent him on a spree, he was lying low, being that much more careful. As long as she didn't give him an opportunity to get her in a deserted location, she'd be fine. There was no reason to panic.

Ella ignored the doubt pushing through and told Logan, "Okay, I'll switch hotels."

The worry lines on his forehead smoothed out

and he gave her a relieved smile that made the inconvenience totally worth it.

"Good," Logan said, heading into the conference room. "Because I'm already driving my sister crazy, calling her every couple of hours. I'm not sure you want me waking you up in the middle of the night, too."

Actually, she kind of did. But not with a phone call.

Clamping her mouth shut, Ella followed him. "Okay. Let's get to work. Maybe we should start by calling your sister? Make sure she doesn't know of anyone around here that Theresa might have unexpectedly decided to meet."

"I'm on it," Logan said, his cell phone already pressed to his ear.

As Ella sat and devoured the rest of her candy bar, she half listened to Logan tell his sister, "No, that's not why I'm calling this time, but I'm glad everything's okay there." He grinned at Ella as if to say, "See, I *am* driving her crazy."

Logan continued to talk to Becky, and Ella

knew she should be listening, but her mind kept wandering. If Theresa hadn't been ambushed on a deserted stretch of road like they'd imagined, then her killer—whoever he was—had grabbed her somewhere else. Not only did they have no idea where that was, but they had no clue how he'd done it, either. Had he lured her out there? It seemed unlikely, unless she knew him. Had she been meeting someone else and the killer had taken advantage of the unexpected opportunity? That, too, seemed unlikely.

The problem was, everything in Ella's profile was based on the idea that they knew certain things as fact. That the killer had tortured and burned Theresa before dumping her body in a location it was unlikely to be found. That he had grabbed her when she was heading in a direct route from Becky's house to the airport.

If they were wrong about where she was grabbed, which they clearly were, then too much of Ella's profile could also be wrong.

Anxiety spiked as she glanced over at Logan,

talking to his sister. The sister she'd promised would be safe if she didn't go anywhere deserted, if she didn't give the killer a chance to ambush her. But if he wasn't ambushing his victims after all...

Ella stood, started to pace. She felt Logan's speculative look and when he ended the call, she preempted his question by saying, "Logan, maybe you should put your sister in protective custody."

He stared at her, his expression probing, as if he was trying to read her mind. "Believe me, if we had the resources, I would. But we don't." He stood, took her hand in his own. "The abduction style isn't the only reason you think the killer would wait to get his victims alone, right?"

Ella bit her lip as her heart rate started to crescendo with her nerves. The nature of her job meant that lives always hung in the balance of how deeply she could get into the killer's head. But this—this panic she was feeling—was why her boss had always kept her away from cases where branding could be involved. Being too personally invested meant she wasn't seeing things objectively. It meant she could be making mistakes.

Ella brought her free hand to her temple. When had this happened? When had she started to care so much about Logan that she couldn't see the case clearly?

"Ella," Logan said softly. "The way the body was dumped, the way the killer stalked Theresa, the way he's still lying low now, they all tell you he wouldn't risk breaking into the mayor's house in a security-conscious neighborhood to make a grab, right?"

"Yes. But, Logan, I'm not right one hundred percent of the time. And profiling isn't magic. People do uncharacteristic things and I can't predict that."

And she didn't think she'd ever be able to forgive herself if she was wrong this time and Logan's little sister paid the price.

Logan squeezed her fingers. "I trust you, Ella. But, believe me, I'm not taking chances with my sister's life. And neither is my family. My dad has already hired her a bodyguard. Becky isn't thrilled about it, but it keeps me from panicking if she doesn't answer my million calls on the first ring."

Ella let out a long breath. "Okay." She looked up into Logan's eyes, and something about his steady demeanor calmed her. "What did Becky say?"

"She didn't know of any exes in the area. And she had called Theresa when she was on her way to the airport because Theresa left a necklace behind. But Theresa told Becky to mail it to her, because she didn't want to miss her flight."

"Huh. So either Theresa was lying or something happened after Becky talked to her that made her change her mind."

Logan shrugged, let go of her hand. "I guess so. Becky and Theresa were close. I have a hard time imagining her lying to my sister, but I can't think of anything that would make her decide at the last minute to skip her flight, either. And neither could Becky. Let me go check the fax machine and see if those call records have come in."

"Great," Ella said, lowering herself into a conference chair as he hurried out of the room. It was hard to muster up a lot of enthusiasm.

Nothing about this case was turning out like she'd expected. And despite the burns, she was beginning to wonder if it was connected to Maggie's case at all.

When Logan returned a minute later and dropped a stack of pages on the table, looking dejected, Ella sat straighter and asked, "Nothing?"

"We got the call records." He gestured to the papers he'd scattered. "But the only calls Theresa got after she left for the airport were two from Becky. That's it."

"Well, what about—"

"No other local calls while she was in Oakville, either." Logan sighed. "It's possible someone followed her from Arkansas and made contact. But it'll take time to track down the rest of the calls she got while she was in town."

He rubbed a hand over his eyes and Ella saw the exhaustion he was trying to hide. Not physical exhaustion so much as emotional.

"I'm not sure which route to take here, Ella. Tracking the phone numbers will likely lead us to the killer if he's someone in her life. But a stranger? For that, we'd probably be better off following up on the people who might've seen Theresa at the gas station. We've got officers on that already, but I want to spend our time on the most likely option. I know I'm putting you on the spot, but what's your professional opinion at this point? Do you still believe we're talking about a serial killer here?"

Did she? Ella pushed back her uncertainty. *Think, Cortez. Think like the killer.*

She might not know how the killer had grabbed Theresa, but she did know what he'd done to her afterward. The burns. The strangulation. The dumping of the body.

Someone from Arkansas might think a marsh was an easy place to dispose of the body, because it was simple to access and the body would sink, disappear in the muck. But what about the logistics? Where would he have carried out the murder? A hotel? How would he have gotten the body out into the marsh? Rented a boat? Would a nonlocal have felt comfortable rowing out among the gators?

And the crime itself. Torture and strangulation could be personal, a vendetta against someone. Or it could be the mark of a serial killer.

But those burns. Whether or not they were brands, they were specific. Part of a fantasy. They weren't about the victim, but about the killer.

Ella felt her confidence returning. "It's a serial killer."

"WE HAVE A WITNESS."

"What?" Ella looked up at Logan as he hurried back to their table at the Blue Dolphin where they'd been eating a lunch so late it might as well have been called dinner. He'd gone outside to answer his phone because the Blue Dolphin was packed and loud, just like it had been the first time he'd brought her here.

Logan hurriedly wrapped the sandwich he'd barely started and Ella did the same, pushing her chair backward.

"That call was from one of the officers who was running down the license plates from the gas station. One of the women who was there not only remembered Theresa, she talked to her."

"What?" Ella's eyes widened. Could this be the break they needed? "What did she say?"

"Come on. I'll tell you in the car." Logan picked up his drink and moved through the crowd toward the door.

Ella followed, her mind working overtime,

imagining all the possibilities. "Well?" she demanded as they got into Logan's Chevy Caprice and he pulled the car out fast.

"The woman said she talked to Theresa inside as Theresa was paying."

"Wait," Ella interrupted. "Why was she paying inside? She used her credit card. Why not pay at the pump?"

Logan glanced at her as he pointed the car in the opposite direction from where they'd headed to check out the highway. "She also bought gum."

"Okay, so what did the witness say? And where are we going?"

"The woman said she overheard Theresa asking for directions and she looked frustrated. The woman helped her with the directions and asked if everything was okay. Theresa told her she was just annoyed because she was going to miss her flight. She was meeting someone."

A dozen questions formed in Ella's mind, but she couldn't seem to ask any of them. Instead, her mouth fell open as she realized what Logan's words meant. She'd been wrong. Very, very wrong. Theresa had probably known her killer.

"Ella?" Logan glanced at her again. "You okay?"

Ella shook herself out of it. "Yeah. Did she say who she was meeting?"

"No. Just that it was a friend. But she did say where she was going. And this is even weirder. She was meeting the person in Huntsville."

"And? Why is that weird?"

"Well, Huntsville *is* in the same general direction as where we ultimately found Theresa's rental, and the gas station where she stopped is along that route. But there's nothing there. It's an old farming community, but it's pretty much abandoned. There are a few old-timers left, and at some point soon, developers will buy up the land and build a mall or something. But right now, it's mostly open land and falling-down barns."

Ella gave him a questioning look as he finally left the Oakville city limits and got onto a country highway, picking up speed. "Sounds like a pretty good place for an abduction and murder, then. So why is it weird? I mean, yes, it's weird that she was meeting someone in the first place, but if she didn't know the area and he did..."

Logan briefly turned to face her, and Ella saw something simmering under the surface she hadn't noticed before. Anger. "Ella, my mom's parents owned a farm out here. It's long been deserted, but we still own the land. And the reason Theresa started talking to this woman is that she was trying to get directions and the woman overheard her. Apparently, she knew my grandparents, so she remembered where they'd lived. And according to her, that's where Theresa was going. She remembers—and thought it was odd—because my grandparents have been dead for ten years."

This case just got stranger and stranger. Ella

tried to digest the new development. "Logan, you said your family were the last people to see Theresa in town before she died, right?"

"Yeah."

"And now this. Maybe this isn't about Theresa at all. Maybe someone's trying to frame you."

Logan pounded a fist against the steering wheel. "You think someone kidnapped—and *tortured*—Theresa to hurt my family?"

Ella rested her head against the seat, clutching the food she'd barely touched. She wasn't hungry anymore, as dread burrowed inside her. "You're right. It doesn't quite fit. It's not a very good frame-up if it was this much of a stretch for us to even find the information. Plus, the burns are personal to him. I know they are. That's not about your family, or even about the victim, really. It's about *him*."

"So, what? This can't be coincidence," Logan said, his knuckles bone white as he squeezed the steering wheel.

"I don't know. Maybe it was part of a lure?

Maybe Theresa thought she was meeting someone from your family there?" Even as she said it, the words sounded far-fetched.

"How? And why? We haven't gone there in years. And Becky was the last person to talk to Theresa, so who would have told her to meet us there? And since she talked to Becky on her way to the airport, why would she go? Why wouldn't she have said something to Becky? And why would she miss her flight to meet us at a deserted farm?"

Ella shook her head, feeling as frustrated as Logan sounded. "I don't know," she said again.

They both fell silent as Logan's Chevy Caprice sped toward the farm. It took a while for the lights of busy neighboring towns to fade, for the land to shift into something that might have once supported farms.

By then, Ella felt the need to admit what they both had to be thinking. "I was wrong, Logan. Whatever the purpose, however this guy got her here, this wasn't a quick ambush. This was a complicated lure. He wasn't waiting for Theresa to take the usual route and then picking out the most suitable place for an ambush."

She shook her head. "Either he knew Theresa personally, or…" A heavy weight seemed to settle on her chest. "This guy is a baiter."

Logan must have caught her change in tone, because as he pulled the car to a stop outside an obviously deserted house, he turned toward her, waiting.

Ella shifted, looking into the green eyes that had tempted her into a supposedly quick dinner and review of a case file only a few days ago. It felt like so much longer. So much had changed in that short time.

And yet, the one thing she'd ultimately come to Oakville for wasn't going to change. This killer *was* a baiter. And Maggie's rapist liked to ambush his victims. They were very different methods, used by different personality types.

She felt an old pain swell up, and her voice

trembled as she told him, "This isn't my shot to catch Maggie's rapist. This is a totally different killer."

Chapter Nine

Logan felt queasy as he picked the lock on his grandparents' old house. It had sat empty for a decade, but his mom couldn't bring herself to sell it. He hadn't been to the house in years, but he had so many good memories here. If they went inside and found evidence that Theresa had died here, it would tarnish all of them.

A gag worked its way up his throat and he swallowed it down, focused on fitting the pick into the old lock. When the lock finally clicked and he pushed the door open, he froze, not wanting to go inside.

Growing up, he'd always felt safe here. Greers had lived in this area going back six generations. And on his mom's side, it had been almost as long. They had history here, and even now, most of the family had stuck around. He'd taken the police job to keep the hometown he loved safe. Now, with Theresa's death, it all felt tainted by something dark and ugly.

Ella squeezed past him. "Why don't you wait here, Logan?" She glanced back at him with understanding in her eyes. "I'll call you if I need you."

"No. I'm coming with you." He just hoped if they found something, he didn't contaminate the scene by throwing up.

With a deep breath, he followed Ella inside. Into the living room where his grandpa's ugly comfortable plaid chair had once sat in the corner, where the doilies his grandma made once covered all the tables. Now it was bare, covered with a thick layer of dust and cobwebs. But no evidence anyone had been through the house recently. At least not in this room.

He followed Ella toward the back of the house,

but it was the same there. To his relief, it looked completely deserted, as if no one had been inside for years.

Ella turned to him.

"Are there any outbuildings on the property?"

"No." Logan studied the house again, remembering the way it had once been, filled with the smell of the cigars his grandpa used to smoke, the smell of his grandma's perfume. Filled with laughter as he and Becky had run down the stairs and out into the backyard. He remembered the sound of his grandma's voice calling after them, admonishing them to slow down, trying to hide the smile in her voice.

The memories faded, leaving behind the image of the empty, dusty house as it was now, as Logan unlocked the back door and stepped outside. The property stretched for miles, but it was fairly flat and unobstructed. Although the area was pretty deserted, it seemed unlikely that someone as smart as this killer would have tortured and murdered Theresa outside.

Logan turned back to Ella. "What do you think?"

"It doesn't look like anyone has been here. Maybe she met the killer here and went with him somewhere else? He might have lured her here, then knocked her out. He probably could have left the car here without attracting attention, then come back for it later. It does seem odd, though. Why here? If he was going to grab her, why not do it on the way to the airport, like we originally suspected? And if he was going to lure her somewhere—if he'd charmed her enough to get her to meet up with him—why bring her here? Why not just meet her wherever he killed her?"

Logan shrugged. "I have no idea. None of this makes any sense. But I don't like it. This feels too personal, this guy picking my grandparents' house. How did he know about it?"

He headed back through the house, ready to lock it up and leave. Even though they'd seen no evidence that Theresa had been here, his nerves were twitching, telling him something about the whole scenario was off. It made him want to get out of there fast, as if he could outrun what had happened to Theresa, somehow undo it.

"Maybe you should call Becky," Ella said as they got back in his car for the return trip to Oakville. "See if she ever mentioned this place to Theresa. Maybe Theresa was the one who suggested meeting here, and not her killer."

Logan nodded, stuck his hands-free device in his ear and dialed. After a short conversation, he told Ella, "Yeah, my sister mentioned the house, but just in talking about my grandparents. They never discussed coming here."

Logan pulled out onto the highway, reaching for the drink he hadn't touched on the way up. The coffee was cold now, but he gulped it down anyway, wanting the caffeine hit. "The more answers we find in this case, the more questions we get. I've investigated a couple of homicides since I made detective, but nothing like this."

Frustration built inside him, together with the fear that this killer was going to outwit him. That he'd never be able to bring the guy to justice. That he'd fail Theresa, fail Becky.

Ella's cool hand sliding behind his neck, kneading the tight muscles there, surprised him. He glanced over at her, and he could tell from the tilt of her head, from the expression in her eyes. She understood exactly how he felt.

He relaxed his shoulders, focused on the road, and let Ella work her magic on his neck. Slowly, he felt himself relax.

He smiled at her. "Thanks."

She removed her hand and unwrapped her sandwich. She took a huge bite, then asked, "Were Becky and Theresa together the whole time she was here?"

"Pretty much. Becky had the week off work, but she did have a few things she had to take care of while Theresa was here. Theresa told her she was going to the beach while Becky was out. It was a couple of hours, tops, both times. I asked Becky about it when I first talked to her after we found Theresa's body."

Ella nodded, looking pensive. "So, it's possible she met someone Becky didn't know about, set up a meeting."

"It's possible," Logan agreed. "But it still seems strange that she wouldn't mention it to Becky. And that she would set up a meeting for *after* her flight was supposed to leave. And if it was arranged at the last minute, how did the guy contact her if he didn't call her? If he ran into her somewhere, then why wouldn't they just drive together?"

"I'm not sure any of this is going to make sense until we figure out why Theresa didn't take that flight."

Logan frowned. "Any ideas on how to do that?"

He felt Ella's eyes on him as she said, "Nothing brilliant, no. We can try to follow up on the beach angle, see if we can find someone who remembers seeing Theresa with a guy. Maybe put out a request to the public for information. You could use your media contact."

"Lyla?" Logan snorted. "We didn't exactly part on the best of terms. I'll talk to her if you think that could work, but I should warn you that she's tenacious. Once she gets hold of something, she doesn't stop chasing it. I can guarantee you that if she has any chance to get back into the police station, she's going straight back to her profiler story."

"Well, that's a risk I'll have to take."

Logan decided he'd talk to Lyla, do his best to convince her to leave Ella out of it, but ultimately, Lyla did whatever Lyla wanted. She always had.

And even trying to leave his personal feelings for Ella aside—which was pretty near impossible—his gut said that if he wanted any chance of nailing this killer, he was going to need her.

As soon as Logan parked at the station, Ella sank low in her seat and he let out a string of curses.

Out front, far enough away from the station that Logan knew Chief Patterson had thrown a fit, but close enough that the station would be in the long shot, was a television crew. Lyla stood by the camera in a fire-engine-red skirt suit, looking as though she'd primped for hours. She had a microphone angled toward Kelly, the woman who'd reported her friend missing a few days ago.

Far from the hungover, terrified mess Kelly had been then, she now looked as if she'd spent all day getting ready to be on TV.

Logan scowled. He'd seen this in other homicide cases, loved ones of victims trying to get media mileage out of their loss, but it always made him feel sick.

As he stepped out of the car, he heard Lyla's voice ringing across the lot, "So, you were led to believe that a serial killer abducted your friend?"

Logan tightened his jaw hard enough that his neck hurt. There was a lot he'd loved about Lyla, but her determination to get the story, which he'd originally found attractive, now grated on his nerves. What she was doing with this case bordered on irresponsible.

Doing his best to ignore it, Logan made a bee-line for the station doors, refusing to look over at the spectacle that was the "news."

He felt Ella close on his heels and he held open the door for her to duck inside. But inside the station wasn't much better.

"I thought your fiancée left town when she left you," Hank O'Connor muttered darkly, as he walked past them.

Logan thought Hank was going to keep walking; but instead he stopped, turned around and poked a finger at Logan's chest. "This *serial killer* angle is getting out of control. Is this your idea of how being a detective works?"

Logan looked down at the beefy finger pointing at him and clenched his fists to keep from reaching up and twisting it until it snapped.

Beside him, Ella took a step forward, getting

Hank's attention. "I've worked with a lot of detectives over the past few years."

Ella's voice was too even, too sweet. Logan shot a questioning look at her.

"The best ones chase down every lead, no matter where it takes them." She pivoted and walked past Hank, calling over her shoulder, "Even if they're not happy about it. Even if it leads to a serial killer."

Hank watched her walk away, then turned back to Logan with a smirk on his face. "I guess I'd cry serial killer, too, if it got me a cute little piece of—"

Logan got in his face fast. "You don't like me, fine. I don't like you much, either. Leave Ella out of it."

Hank was a big guy. In a brawl, he'd have a definite advantage over Logan. But as Logan stared him down, fury in his eyes, Hank nodded and backed up.

"Sorry," he choked out, not sounding particularly sincere. But then he rolled his massive shoulders and added, "Whoever this killer is, let's just find him, fast." He gestured out the doors to where the camera crew was packing up. "Because the last thing we need is more panic."

Logan held out his hand. He and Hank would probably never be friends, but they did have to work together.

Hank looked at it skeptically for a minute, then locked his beefy hand around it and shook. "So far, we've got nothing on Laurie's whereabouts. I still think she's sleeping it off somewhere, but..." He glanced back in the direction Ella had gone, then added, "We've run out of places to look. If you need help running something down, let me know. I want to find this girl alive."

Logan nodded. "Believe me, so do I."

He sighed as Hank walked away, because as much as he hoped Hank was right about Laurie, he was banking on Ella's expertise and his own gut here. And both told him that Laurie had met the same fate as Theresa. That if they found Laurie at all, it wasn't going to be alive.

Forcing aside that gruesome thought, Logan made his way to the conference room. Inside, he saw Ella hunched over the table, writing frantically.

"What are you working on?"

She looked up, blinking until she seemed to focus on him. "Questions for the officers searching for Laurie. They're still talking to locals and tourists at the bars and anywhere else Laurie might have been, right?"

Logan dropped into the chair next to her. "They are, but it's not going anywhere. They don't have any leads. You have some new ideas on that?"

"Kind of. I think we should have them ask anyone who talked to Laurie while she was here if she ever mentioned meeting someone. And I think the officers should also ask every one of them if they ever saw Theresa with anyone besides Becky."

Her lips pursed, and her expression turned serious, intense. "Given what was going on outside, I'm having second thoughts about involving the media in this. But since the officers are still canvassing on Laurie, let's use what we've learned about Theresa today."

"Okay, that makes sense." Logan reached across her for his laptop, which he'd left in the conference room during their drive out to his grandparents' farm. "While you do that, I'm going to track down blue vans."

"Thanks."

Ella picked up her pen again and got back to work, but not before he saw something spark in her eyes. Logically, she might not have been sure about it, but he knew she felt that the van was connected. And so far, Logan trusted Ella's instincts more than those of any other law enforcement officer he'd ever met.

She was smart. And she was familiar with this kind of killer, far more than he'd ever be, far more than he ever wanted to.

Logan powered up his laptop, intent on locating every blue van within a fifty-mile radius. He'd go door to door if he had to, but he wasn't stopping until he'd checked out every single person who owned one.

ELLA HAD NEVER thought of herself as a jealous person. But as she strode into her new hotel across town and spotted Lyla lounging in the lobby, obviously planning to ambush her, that emotion bubbled up, strong and sour.

It was late and she was exhausted. She didn't have the energy to deal with a typical reporter right now, let alone Logan's supermodel-impersonator ex-fiancée.

Ignoring Lyla, who'd jumped to her feet, Ella tiredly told the man behind the check-in desk, "I need a room. Detective Greer called ahead."

As Lyla crowded up next to her, Ella was suddenly glad she hadn't let Logan come inside with her. That would've been a career-killing story for both of them.

Logan had driven her to her old hotel to get her bag and check out, arranged a room for her here, and then stopped the car in front of the lobby doors. The hopeful look in his green eyes had told her that, with the slightest encouragement, he'd park and come in with her.

A shiver of desire raced through her veins. She'd almost done it. Almost thrown caution aside and invited him to her room. Almost told him to forget the hotel entirely and take her back to his house. But a tiny thread of sanity had prevailed and she'd gotten out of the car, fast. And alone.

Because as good as she knew they'd be together, with every day in his company, Ella was becoming increasingly certain that this was about more than lust for her. Certain that after one night of passion with Logan, she'd spend the rest of her life looking for anything that could possibly compare. And coming up short.

"Here you go, ma'am," the hotel employee told her, handing her a key card. "Room—"

"I got it," Ella said, looking at the number on the key card. She didn't want Lyla knowing her room number and harassing her there.

As she turned away from the desk, stupidly hoping that if she just ignored Lyla, the woman would go away, Lyla stepped into stride beside her.

"I'm Lyla Evans. I've been reporting on the serial killer case." She held out a manicured hand that Ella ignored.

"O-kay," Lyla said in response to the snub. "Look, I know you probably don't want to talk to a reporter, but—"

"No, I don't." Ella cut her off, stabbing the Up button on the hotel elevator.

But when the elevator arrived, Lyla got in with her.

Ella threw her an exasperated look, aware that she was being rude, but not able to help herself. "Are you planning to camp out outside my hotel room? I have no comment on the investigation."

"You're the profiler, right?" Lyla pressed anyway. "From the FBI?"

"I have no comment."

Lyla gave her a camera-ready, practiced smile and stepped in front of her so Ella couldn't ignore her. "Don't you think the residents of Oakville have a right to know if they're being stalked by a serial killer?"

Ella raised an eyebrow. "Oh, I've seen the press. I think they're plenty scared. If you were really interested in safety, you'd be coordinating with the police, not chasing headlines."

Lyla blinked, took a step back. "The police aren't all that interested in cooperating."

The sigh that had been building in Ella's chest broke free. "They might have been, if you'd approached this differently. I'm sorry, I just don't have any comment."

As the elevator reached her floor, Ella got off, half expecting Lyla to follow. But she heard the door shut again, and when she glanced behind her, Lyla wasn't there.

Her relief was short-lived, though. Her cell phone rang, and when she looked at the read-out, she saw the call was from her boss.

She quickly let herself into her room, dropped her bag on the floor, then took a deep breath and picked up. "Isabella Cortez."

"Where are you, Ella?" From the pissed-off tone of her boss's voice, she could tell he already knew the answer.

Dread sank hard and fast to the pit of her stomach and Ella sat on the edge of the bed. She might be about to lose her job. At least by sitting down she'd do less damage if she fainted.

"I'm in Florida, sir. I'm consulting on a case unofficially, as a civilian."

Her boss released a succinct string of curses that told her that answer wasn't acceptable. "You work for the FBI, Ella. You can't consult unofficially."

"Sir, I thought this might have been connected

to my friend's case. Now I'm pretty sure it's not, but—"

"You thought it was about the Fishhook Rapist?"

"Yes." Her boss knew how important solving that case was to her, how it had led her to the Bureau in the first place.

"Ella, you're a good agent. I like having you on my team. Don't screw around with your career by taking side jobs."

"Sir—"

"You're scheduled to be on vacation through next week?"

"Yes, sir."

He sighed. "Fine. I'm probably too busy to be watching every little piece of Florida news anyway."

"Thank—" Ella started, but he cut her off.

"Just get the TV stations to stop talking about FBI involvement. You're there as a civilian, which is nonsense, but the Bureau isn't taking any responsibility for this. And I don't care where the investigation stands at the end of next week. You get back here, or there won't be a position for you to return to. Understand?"

"Yes, sir," Ella said meekly.

After he hung up, she closed her eyes and dropped backward so she was lying across the bed.

She had just over a week to find Theresa's killer. And she had a very bad feeling it wouldn't be nearly enough time.

Chapter Ten

"I don't think this case is connected to Maggie's."

In response to her announcement, there was a long pause on the other end of the phone.

Ella leaned back against her hotel headboard. California was three hours earlier, and knowing Scott, he hadn't been sleeping at 10:00 p.m. He was either out looking for a woman to charm, or more likely, he'd already found one.

"Hang on a sec," Scott said finally. She could hear him moving around, then a minute later, he asked, "Are you sure?"

"I'm not positive yet. I'm going to try to talk to the medical examiner in the morning, but I think this killer is a baiter."

"Different MO," Scott agreed.

He didn't sound disappointed, just resigned, because a decade was a long time to keep hoping the Fishhook Rapist would finally be caught. Every year, that horrible anniversary rolled around and she, Maggie and Scott gathered together and tried to distract each other, dreading the news the next morning.

"I'm sorry," Ella choked out, mortified to hear the tears in her voice. "I really thought it was him. I really thought I had a chance to get this guy."

"It's not your fault, kiddo," Scott said, and Ella smiled at the nickname he'd had for her since she'd first moved to town and met him and Maggie.

Scott was only a year older, but he had two younger sisters and even before Maggie's rape, he'd taken that role very seriously. He'd quickly extended his big brother protective role to her, too.

Most of the time, these days, she found it

funny. After all, she was an armed FBI agent. She was long past needing a big brother to look after her. But once in a while, it was comforting, reminding her of everything that was good about growing up in their small town.

"I know." Ella sighed wearily. "But I just wanted to end this."

"I know you did," Scott said. "I did, too. But sooner or later, he's going to mess up and he'll get caught."

"I hope so."

"What else is going on?" Scott asked.

"What do you mean?"

"Come on, I hear it in your voice. Something else is upsetting you."

In spite of everything, Ella felt herself smile. Her family might have pulled away since she'd joined the Bureau, but Scott and Maggie never let her down. "My boss heard about me coming down here. I'm getting some heat for it."

"Well, I wouldn't worry too much about that. Your boss knows how good you are—he'll get over it. And if the case isn't connected, then you can come join us in California, lie on the beach for a week and relax before you have to go back and deal with him."

Even knowing Scott couldn't see her, Ella fidgeted. "I can't."

"Why not?"

"Well, the police…they need my help on this."

Scott snorted with laughter. "You are such a bad liar."

"I *can* help with this case."

"That's not what I mean and you know it, Ella. What else is going on?"

"Uh…"

"It's that guy I saw you with at the airport, isn't it?" Even over the phone, Ella could sense Scott's grin. "Don't tell me you finally found someone who's actually worth your time?"

"Yeah, and he happens to live about a thousand miles from me."

"So what?"

"Well, that's a long way to travel for a dinner

date," Ella tried to joke, but it ended up sounding dejected instead of funny.

"Ella. People have long-distance relationships all the time."

"Yeah, well, I can't even make them work when the guy lives down the hall from me."

"Maybe that's because you never wanted to badly enough before," Scott suggested with a seriousness in his voice that told Ella he and Maggie had talked about this.

Was he right? Was it really that simple?

Ella glanced in the mirror across from her bed, at the tired eyes staring back. Her job was important to her, but it wasn't her whole life. Had she never made time for her relationships before because she hadn't found the right person?

"Hey, kiddo, don't let me upset you," Scott said, making her realize she'd gone silent for too long. "Just think about it."

"You're right," Ella agreed. "And I will."

Hanging up the phone, Ella slid under the

covers and closed her eyes, an image of Logan grinning at her, those green eyes sparkling, instantly filling her mind. Maybe she was foolish to keep resisting the pull between them. Maybe they *could* make something work.

She smiled as she drifted off to sleep.

"WHAT HAPPENED WITH you and Lyla?"

Ella cringed as she finished buckling herself into the passenger seat in Logan's car. Had she really just asked that? She'd been thinking it, but she'd intended to ask about talking to the medical examiner regarding Theresa. She couldn't believe that had come out instead.

Before she could backtrack, laugh lines appeared beside Logan's eyes and he said, "Good morning to you, too, Ella."

"Sorry." Ella felt herself redden. "She was waiting at the hotel last night and I—"

Logan twisted in his seat to face her. "She was *what*?"

"She wanted an interview."

Logan swore under his breath. "I'm sorry about that, Ella."

"Yeah, and about what was on the news... My boss called last night."

Logan actually looked a little queasy as he asked, "Do you have to leave?"

"No, my boss is a good guy. He's giving me some leeway on this."

Logan's shoulders dropped, and he seemed relieved as he nodded and pulled away from the hotel.

"But he's going to be pissed if he keeps seeing mention of the FBI in the news, because my involvement is definitely not sanctioned. Is there anything you can do?"

"I'll take care of it."

Ella willed herself not to get any more flushed than she probably was as she admitted, "I was kind of rude to Lyla yesterday. She's probably not going to want to do me any favors."

Logan's eyes narrowed as he headed in the direction of the police station. "I'd have been

rude to her, too, if she'd been waiting to ambush me for a story."

"Yeah, but I'm usually more professional.
I think just knowing about your history with
her sort of…" Ella threw her hands up. "I don't
know. Sorry."

Logan glanced at her quickly before returning
his attention to the road, but that look told her
he was surprised. And maybe a little pleased.

"That's been over for years. Believe me, right
now, there's no one else." He added softly, "You
don't have any competition."

The heat in Ella's cheeks turned to fire. What
did he mean by "right now"? It was the perfect
opening for what she'd considered asking him
all last night—whether there was a chance for
them beyond her time in Florida. But her mouth
didn't seem to work.

Logan glanced at her again, probably waiting
for a response, and still, Ella felt frozen.

She'd never thought of herself as a coward.
When it came to the job, back in the gangs unit,

she had a reputation for always wanting to be on the first team through the door.

Even on her worst day in the unit, when she'd been shot and was bleeding out on the street, she hadn't done the sensible thing and played dead. Instead, she'd dragged herself farther into the line of fire, trying to get to her partner, not knowing it was already too late. She'd gotten her partner's killer before he'd gotten her, and then she'd put a tourniquet around her own leg while she waited for backup. The FBI had given her a letter of commendation for her actions that day. She hadn't thought of herself as a coward then.

But apparently, when it came to matters of the heart, she was a big wimp.

Buck up, Cortez.

She took a deep breath, but then Logan was saying in his back-to-business tone, "Last night I finished putting together a list of locals who own blue vans. I thought we could run them down today."

"Oh. Okay. Great." Ella felt a mingling of relief and disappointment at her missed opportunity.

"I included anyone from surrounding towns with blue vans, too. The list isn't very long."

"Well, file that in the good news department."

"No kidding," Logan said. "I figured we could run down the names together and interview anyone who looks like they could fit your profile."

"Sounds good. I'd also like to talk to the ME who did Theresa's autopsy."

"Sure. I can call him. Why?"

"I want to ask him about the burns." She wanted to confirm, once and for all, whether there was any chance this was connected to Maggie's rapist. She didn't think so anymore, but until she had a definitive expert opinion, she was going to wonder. And if it wasn't connected, she could stop thinking about Maggie's case every time she tried to analyze this perp's possible next move.

"Okay." Logan shifted, took his cell phone

from his pocket, and handed it to her. "He's in there. Just pull up ME in the Contacts."

Ella raised an eyebrow. "You have the ME on speed dial? That's just sad."

Logan let out a short bark of laughter. "It's easier than having to look it up whenever I get a homicide case. My Contacts list is a Who's Who of Oakville law enforcement." He gave her a goofy grin. "I even have the mayor on speed dial."

Ella rolled her eyes, then called the ME. When he picked up, she told him, "This is Isabella Cortez. I'm consulting—"

"From the FBI," he interrupted. "I watch the news. What do you need?"

Ella grimaced. She definitely had to get Logan to talk to Lyla for her. "I wanted to ask about the burns on Theresa's body. Is there any possibility that they could have been branding?"

The ME went silent and Ella realized she was holding her breath. All her profiling instincts told her the new development in Theresa's case meant it wasn't connected to Maggie, but she found herself actually hoping she was wrong.

Finally, the ME said, "The body sustained significant damage when it was in the marsh. But my professional judgment is no, the burns weren't made from a brand. I suspect they were made by literally holding a flame to the skin."

Ella's lips curled in distaste, but she had to ask, "Are you positive it's not a brand? Even the one on her neck? The shape kind of reminded me of a hook."

"Hmm. It does look a bit that way, doesn't it? If I had to make a guess, I'd say the shape is because the flame caught her hair before it was put out. The burns looked controlled, as if this woman's killer was trying to inflict specific damage, burn specific areas. If that's the case, it probably wasn't intentional, but I suspect the fire got away from him briefly, which would explain the way that particular burn hooks upward, toward the skull. It's definitely not a brand, though. I can tell you that."

Ella slumped, as disappointment gathered in her chest. "Thanks."

As she hung up, Logan asked, "It's not connected to your friend's case?"

"No."

The word came out slightly strangled, and Logan reached out his hand, folding it tightly around hers.

She gave him a half smile. "Because we now suspect baiting, I didn't believe it was connected anymore, but..."

"You wanted the chance to bring him to justice. I understand, Ella."

"But the fact that it's not a brand tells us something, too." Ella considered what the ME had told her, thinking out loud. "The burns were localized, specific. Were they just a means of torture or something more?"

She looked over at Logan as he parked the Chevy Caprice in the station lot. "Do you know anyone around here who's badly burned?"

Logan shook his head. "No. Why? Do you

think the killer is burning his victims because he's scarred from burns himself?"

Ella thought about the autopsy photos she'd studied the day Logan had come to see her in Virginia. "Maybe. A brand is a sign of ownership. But a burn is different. It could be a way for the killer to torture his victims, especially if that's his end goal. But it's possible he picked fire because of a connection to his own life."

She stepped out of the car and followed Logan into the station. "It's really hard to say for sure at this point."

With only one body, only one victim conclusively tied to this killer, it was difficult to form a complete profile.

And without more to go on, and with a killer this careful and controlled, it was going to be nearly impossible to find him.

EVERY OFFICER IN the station looked weary, frustrated and dejected.

As Logan and Ella walked through the bull-pen, Logan's colleagues looked back at him with bloodshot eyes. Most of them were running on caffeine now, and were well past the point of being fueled by the hope of finding Laurie hungover and apologetic. At this point, she'd been missing too long.

Still, Logan knew most of them didn't believe she'd been grabbed by a serial killer. Some theorized she was hitchhiking home without Kelly, since she'd told people at the bars she was leaving. A few thought she'd shacked up with some local. Others thought she'd gone to the beach after the bar and drowned. It wouldn't be the first time something like that happened to a spring breaker, and the ocean could take a body as easily as the gators in the marsh.

By now, most of the force was resigned to the idea that something bad had happened to her, but none were willing to make the jump to serial killer. They just didn't want to believe serial killings could happen in Oakville.

As Logan bypassed the bullpen for the conference room, with Ella in tow, he wondered if it was time to give up on trying to track Theresa's movements. Maybe they'd have better luck tracking Laurie.

Before he could suggest it to Ella, she asked, "Where's that list of blue van owners?"

Logan booted up his laptop. "I've got it on here."

"Great. Are rentals on there, too? From the closest airports?"

Logan sent her a disbelieving look. "I'm not a miracle worker, Ella. We can get those, but it'll take longer. And I figured locals were our best bet."

"They are."

Ella settled into the chair next to him, making him want to scoot even closer. Making him want to resume the conversation they'd been having in the car, the one that started with her basically admitting she was jealous of his ex-fiancée and ended with him looking like a fool by trying to get her to admit to more.

But he was all too happy to look like a fool if it meant Ella would let him back into her hotel room, pull him down on her bed again.

"But even if Theresa's murder isn't connected to Maggie's case," she continued, "it could still be someone who's been in the area long enough to scout it out for killing, someone who plans to move on. It could be why you don't have any other bodies or reports of missing persons."

Logan frowned. He'd assumed they'd found no other bodies because the gators had taken care of the evidence for the killer, but Ella was right about missing persons. The only missing person report they'd had in the past year was Laurie.

Was he as crazy as his chief and the rest of the force seemed to think? Was he imagining a serial killer here?

Logan forced back his doubt. If he was imagining it, Ella wouldn't have come here in the first place.

"If we're talking about tracking down rental vans from several months back, that would be a big project. And if we're talking about someone who drove here in his own vehicle, we'll never find it. If this guy isn't a local, I think the van angle is a dead end."

"Well, let's see who we've got," Ella said, but he could hear in her voice that she'd begun to feel as dejected as his fellow officers.

"Okay." Logan pulled up the list he'd run, reminding himself to be impartial. He was probably going to know everyone on it. And he couldn't think of anyone in Oakville he'd peg as a murderer.

"The first name on the list is Jane Franklin." He tried not to snort as he showed Ella the DMV picture of Jane. "She's fifty-seven years old, married, with two kids and one grandchild."

"Does either kid still live at home? Would one of them have access to the van?"

"No."

"Okay. Who's next? We're looking for a man."

"Most of the list is women," Logan told her.

"Okay." He could hear the frustration in her voice as she asked, "Do any of them have men in their lives who might be driving the vans?"

"Besides one widow, they're all married—"

"What about sons? Our killer isn't married."

Logan read over the names again, thinking. "All except one of these women have kids who are too young to drive." He tapped his finger against one name, even as he shook his head. "Marissa Evans."

"Evans?"

"Yeah, Lyla's mom. Lyla moved up north a few years back, but her family lives one town over. And her brother still lives at home. He's in his late twenties, but he's autistic."

"Is he high-functioning? Does he drive?"

"Yes. And yes. But—"

"Is he socially awkward?"

"Yes. But I've known Joe a long time. He's not a killer."

Ella's lips pursed and he could tell she was trying to be diplomatic when she told him, "In my job, I see a lot of cases where killers hid their impulses so well that no one close to them suspected."

"I get that, Ella, but trust me on this one. Joe isn't a killer. There's no way."

She didn't look convinced, and for a minute she seemed about to argue, but finally she nodded and said, "Who else do you have?"

"Two single men on the list of blue van owners." He held up the first picture. "Adam Pawlter. Sixty-six years old. Unmarried."

Ella studied the picture a minute, then shook her head. "The guy we're looking for would be younger. Does Adam have kids?"

"No, but he took in his sister's son after she died."

"Does he still live at home?"

"I don't know. I think Marshall was his name, but I barely remember him. He works for Adam in his shrimping business, but I doubt he still lives with Adam."

"How old is he? Can you check his information?"

"Hang on." Logan pulled up the station's database, looking for anyone named Marshall, then shook his head. "No criminal record." He stood and stuck his head out the door, calling into the bullpen, "Hey, Hank, you know Adam Pawlter, right?"

Hank ambled over, scarfing down a burger on his lunch break. "Yeah, he lives next door to my aunt. Why?"

"Does his nephew still live at home?"

"Marshall? The guy's in his thirties. He has his own place."

"Okay. Thanks."

Hank's eyes narrowed. "Why?"

"Just running down a lead."

"On Adam and Marshall? They're both

nice guys. And hard workers. You ever tried shrimping?"

Logan sighed, not wanting to get into an argument. "No. Look, it's not on them specifically. We're running down anyone who owns a blue van."

"Oh." Hank frowned. "This something the rest of us should be on, too?"

Logan lowered his voice. "It's a long shot."

He absolutely believed Ella when she said there was a problem with the blue van that had followed her. But the truth was, Ella was a beautiful woman in a town still filled to capacity with drunken spring breakers, even after the exodus that happened when news of a potential serial killer hit. Whoever had killed Theresa probably wasn't the only creep in town.

Seeing a blue van in the surveillance footage was suspicious, but it didn't explain why Theresa was there in the first place. Because something had sent her toward Huntsville instead of to the airport that day, and whatever it was, it happened before she showed up at the gas station.

"Okay," Hank said into the silence. "Let me know if you get anything you want help on."

"Thanks." He was surprised that the truce between him and Hank had lasted so long.

It must have shown in his voice, because Hank said, "Look, man, I've been thinking. I know I always hassle you about how you got the job, like a lot of the other guys do. But I realized it doesn't matter. Because you do the work." Hank shrugged. "Truth is, the chief shouldn't have one detective working by himself anyway. I'm lobbying for him to add a new detective position."

Hank grinned and added, "So, put in a good word, would you?" Then he shoved the other half of his sandwich in his mouth and wandered back into the bullpen.

Logan shook his head as he returned to the conference room. Hank O'Connor wanted to be his partner. If today was a day for miracles, maybe they'd find something useful in the van lead, after all.

"Who else do we have?" Ella asked as he sat back down.

The look in her eyes told him she'd overheard him call this a long shot, but apparently she wasn't going to make an issue of it. Maybe she even agreed.

"One more name. Sean Fink. Thirty-six. Unmarried, no kids. Lives here in Oakville."

"Tell me about him. Is he socially awkward?"

Logan laughed. "Sean? No. That guy tries to be the life of every party. He's not married because he thinks he's still in college, on perpetual spring break."

"Hmm." Ella frowned at his computer, then glanced at him, frustration all over her face. "It doesn't sound like anyone fits."

"Maybe the guy who followed you wasn't connected," Logan suggested, his instincts telling him it might have been Sean following her, hoping to pick her up.

"Maybe not." Ella looked up at the ceiling, as though she might find the answer there, then back at him. "I'm not sure where to search next."

Chapter Eleven

Logan rubbed the back of his neck as he stood on the stoop of the Evans family home. He hadn't been here in two years, since he'd taken the promotion to detective and Lyla had moved away from Oakville, ending their engagement.

Beside him, Ella kept shooting quick glances his way, as if he wouldn't notice. She looked almost as uncomfortable as he felt.

But he'd promised her they would interview any man who fit the basic criteria of her profile who also had access to a blue van. And Joe Evans was on that list.

When the door opened, Lyla's mom looked

surprised, then pleased, to see him. Then she noticed Ella and confusion flitted across her face.

Finally, she recovered and gave him a hug that made him feel like a jerk for being here at all.

"Logan. It's nice to see you again. How's your family?"

"They're doing okay, Mrs. Evans." He gestured to Ella. "This is Ella Cortez. She's working with me on a case."

Lyla's mom nodded at her. "Ella, nice to meet you." Then, her attention returned to Logan, her features hardening. "You're here about a case?"

"I'm sorry, but we'd like to talk to Joe."

Mrs. Evans instantly stiffened. "Why?"

"I can't get into details, but we need to ask him a couple of questions."

Her jaw was tight, and he could see all her motherly instincts to protect coming to life. Lyla and her mother looked nothing alike—Lyla was fair like her father while her mom and brother had olive-toned skin and dark hair. But Lyla had gotten her fierce drive as well as her softer side from her mother.

"He's not in any trouble," Logan said quietly. He knew Joe, and he would've bet his badge that Lyla's brother wasn't involved. But he couldn't taint his investigation by ignoring leads simply because he knew the people.

Mrs. Evans narrowed her eyes, obviously trying to read his real intentions, but finally agreed, "Okay. I'm staying while you talk to him, though. And if I don't like the questions, you're leaving, Logan."

"I understand, Mrs. Evans."

She frowned, then stood back and let him and Ella inside. They followed her through the familiar house where he'd come with Lyla countless times during their three-year relationship and into the den, where Joe was sitting.

Joe didn't look up when they entered the room, but Logan hadn't expected him to. He sat down next to Lyla's brother and said, "Hi, Joe."

Joe looked at him, blinked a few times. "Hi, Logan."

He didn't seem either happy or upset to see him, but Logan didn't allow that lack of response to bother him despite the three years he'd tried to befriend Lyla's brother. He knew Joe's autism meant he didn't process the world in the same way as others, didn't feel or show emotions in the same way. But that didn't mean he didn't have them. And it definitely didn't mean he could have killed Theresa or anyone else. Joe might have been different, but once you got to know him, got past his social awkwardness, he was a sweet guy.

Ella sat quietly on the chair across from them, letting him take the lead, while Lyla's mom stood in the doorway, watching carefully.

"Joe, I know we haven't seen each other in a while, but I just wanted to ask you a few questions, okay?"

"Two years, four months, one day," Joe said.

"Two years, four months and one day since Lyla moved away."

Logan nodded, knowing without calculating the time himself that Joe was right. "That is a long time."

Joe shrugged, staring ahead of him at some spot on the carpet. "What are your questions?"

"I wanted to ask about your mom's van. You drive it sometimes, don't you?"

"Yes. I drive it to work some days. Some days, Mom drives me and sometimes I take myself to work."

"Have you driven the van anywhere else in the past few weeks?" Logan glanced at Lyla's mom as he asked the question, but she didn't react to it. She just crossed her arms over her chest.

"I took it for ice cream Thursday of last week at eight p.m. And I drove to the movies on Saturday, two weeks ago, for a six o' clock movie. *Indiana Jones* was playing at the Retro."

Logan smiled. The Retro was the theater in

town that played old movies, usually classics. It was decked out to look like a theater from decades ago, with red velvet curtains across the screen and everything. He and Lyla had gone with Joe a handful of times when they were dating.

"Did you take the van anywhere else in the last few weeks?"

Joe shook his head, still not looking at Logan.

"Okay, Joe." Logan stood. "That's all I needed to ask you about. It was nice to see you."

"Wait," Ella interrupted, leaning forward in her seat. "Joe, have you been watching the news?"

Lyla's mom took a step closer, and Logan watched her, telling her with his eyes that it was okay.

Joe looked at Ella, then back at the floor. "Sometimes I watch the news. If Mom or Dad has it on."

"Have you heard about the woman in the marsh?"

Joe's mouth turned downward, making him look sad and childlike. "Somebody hurt her."

"Yes," Ella said, "Somebody did."

Lyla's mom opened her mouth, probably to stop the questioning, but Ella stood and said, "That's all we needed."

"Okay," Joe said. "Bye."

"Bye, Joe." Logan briefly felt nostalgic. He and Lyla hadn't been able to make it work, but underneath the career-minded reporter had been a good person, with a great family. He wouldn't have gone back and made a different decision, but he wished things had ended better.

Across from him, Ella—the woman who had recently taken hold of his heart and refused to let go—said, "Thanks for helping us out, Joe."

Joe nodded at Ella, then picked up the remote and turned on the TV.

As Lyla's mom led them back to the door, she said, "Good luck with your case, Logan."

"Thanks, Mrs. Evans."

She glanced over at Ella, who was making her

way to his Chevy Caprice, then back to him. "I guess I'd hoped, when you showed up..." She shrugged. "Lyla is happy up north, with her new job. She's dating someone nice." She paused and finally added, "Your girl seems nice, too."

Logan felt himself flush. "She's not—"

"You can't fool an old lady," Mrs. Evans interrupted. "Goodbye, Logan." She closed the door before he could reply.

When he got into the car, Ella said softly, "They're nice people."

Logan nodded. "Yeah, they are." He started the car. "Let's go talk to Sean Fink and Adam Pawlter's nephew."

Ella was silent as they drove toward the Pawlter house, but Logan could practically hear her thinking.

"What's on your mind?"

She turned to face him, but didn't hold his gaze. "Nothing. Just that Joe doesn't fit the profile, I guess."

He could tell there was more, but since he suspected it had to do with Lyla, he didn't ask.

Instead, he maneuvered up to a small weathered house nestled among brand-new condos. The city of Newton was being developed fast, so fast sometimes it barely looked familiar to Logan, even though he'd spent his entire life nearby. "This is Adam Pawlter's place," he said as he parked.

Ella looked surprised. "I thought we were talking to his nephew."

"We can, but Adam's the one with the van. And I don't know Marshall's last name—he's Adam's sister's kid—so we'd have to get his address from Adam anyway." Logan hopped out and headed to the door, hoping this interview would go better than the last one. If nothing else, at least it would be easier.

Ella followed more slowly, gazing around curiously.

"Hank told me developers tried to buy up this

whole area. I guess Adam was the only one who wouldn't sell."

He knocked sharply on the door, and had almost given up when it finally opened. Logan had a vague recollection of Adam Pawlter, but the man standing in front of him didn't match his memory.

Once, he'd been tall and sturdy, as if he belonged on a ship, out shrimping. Now, he was frail and hunched over, and he looked years older than he actually was.

"Sir, I'm Detective Logan Greer, Oakville PD. I wanted to ask you a few questions."

Adam turned to Ella and she held out her hand. "Ella Cortez. I'm consulting with the Oakville Police Department."

Adam leaned against the door frame. "And you want to talk to me?" he rasped. "About what?"

"We just need to ask you a few questions about your van," Logan replied.

Adam's eyes narrowed and his mouth twisted

in a scowl. "Way to sidestep the real question, son." He produced a hacking cough, then stepped back. "And I remember you, Logan. You kids used to come out to our beaches."

Logan smiled. "A long time ago."

"Come on in. I need to sit down anyway." He turned, leading them into his house, which was dimly lit and cluttered with boxes.

"I figured I'd do some of the work myself," Adam said, gesturing to the boxes as he sat down on his couch, by an oxygen tank. "I've got lung cancer. Aggressive. Figured there was no need to leave Marshall to deal with all my stuff when I was gone." He heaved a sigh. "That boy's already been through all of this once, losing his parents when he was just twelve. Happened on vacation, too, poor kid. He had to wait there while I drove up to North Carolina to get him. Took years to get him out of his shell afterward. And now, he's watching me go, too."

"I'm so sorry—" Logan started.

Adam waved his hand in the air. "I smoked

for too many years. Let's not dwell on it. What do you need to know about my van?"

Beside him, Ella spoke up. "Where's the van now?"

"Marshall took it to the docks."

"Marshall…?" Ella prompted.

Adam's eyes narrowed, but he replied, "My nephew. Marshall Jennings. He's always worked for me, but now he'll take over the company. He picked up the van early this morning, left his car here. The pink shrimp season just started."

Logan nodded. Being local, he knew about the fishing industries. "Does he borrow it often?"

Something flashed in Adam's eyes. "Well, now he'll have to, won't he? Since I can't work anymore."

There was an uncomfortable pause, then Ella asked, "Does anyone else drive it?"

"Sure. Everyone on my crew has driven that thing at one point or another."

"Your crew?" Ella asked.

"For my shrimping company. I've got a crew

of seven. I bought the van for work, so that's what we use it for."

"Does anyone drive it outside work hours?"

Adam's jaw jutted out and he stared down at Ella's shoes. "Nope. It's for transporting our haul. Doesn't even have seats in the back, and it smells like shrimp, so I don't think anyone would want to."

"Are you sure?"

He looked up at her, anger flashing in his eyes. "Of course I'm sure."

"And what time do your men go out in the morning? Do they all stick together?" Ella asked.

Logan knew exactly what she was wondering—whether one of them could have snuck off before work started and used the shrimping boat to dump a body. But Logan knew Adam's boat was too big to go into the marsh. If one of his crew was responsible, he hadn't used the shrimping boat.

"What do you mean, *stick together*?" Adam

scowled at Logan, raising his eyebrows as if the question was stupid. "They go out on the ocean together, of course."

"Can we get a list of people who work for you, sir?" Logan asked.

Adam let out another long, hacking cough. "I don't think so."

"Why not?"

"Because you still haven't told me what this is about, and I don't like the implication that one of my guys is doing something wrong. They're all solid workers. Every one of them has worked for me forever." Adam coughed again, violently, then reached for his oxygen tank. "Please show yourself out."

"Sir—" Logan started.

"I want you out! Go!" Adam fumbled with his oxygen, pressing the mask over his nose and mouth.

Logan waited until Adam was breathing without it before he said, "Okay. Sorry to bother you, sir."

He followed Ella out the door and as soon as they were back in his car, Ella said, "Well, *someone* is using that van."

Logan frowned back at her. "Maybe. I don't remember Adam all that well, but I do know he was always ornery. Plus, everyone in three counties probably knows what case I'm investigating by now, so I'm sure he's not happy with what my questions implied." He started the car. "Ready to talk to Sean Fink?"

"Well, we're on such a roll. Why not?"

Logan grinned as he pulled back onto the street for the short drive to Oakville and Sean's house. "You're a good partner, Ella." Logan winked at her. "And a lot prettier than Hank O'Connor."

He'd expected a laugh—or at least an eye roll—but when he glanced over at her, she looked pensive. "What did I say?"

"Nothing. You're a good partner, too."

Her tone was serious, and just when he realized she might be talking about something other than the case, she added, "But I'm not sure you ever want to let Hulking Hank hear you say his name in the same sentence as the word *pretty*."

Logan snorted. "I bet he'd like that nickname, though. Hulking Hank."

"Probably."

Logan glanced over at her, trying to read her, but for once, he genuinely couldn't tell what she was thinking. Before he could ask, he spotted someone leaving a house up ahead, and he hit the brakes, jerked the gearshift into park and hopped out. "Sean!"

The thirty-six-year-old spun toward them, surprise flashing across his features. He strolled over and well before Ella stepped out of the car and Sean reached them, Logan could tell he was drunk. He checked his watch. It was barely noon.

"Logan," Sean said. "How's it hanging?"

Sean had been a year ahead of him, but they'd gone to school together, played high school football together. They'd never really been friends, though, and Logan's dislike of the man ratcheted up a notch as Sean grinned at Ella and actually licked his lips.

"Hi, there," Sean said, sticking out his hand in Ella's direction. "I'm Sean Fink."

Ella shook his hand briskly. "Ella Cortez."

Sean nodded, holding on to Ella's hand too long. "You're the FBI girl, aren't you?" He grinned at her again, the kind of smile that had probably worked for him in his twenties, picking up women in bars, but Logan couldn't believe he still used it. "I like a woman who knows her way around a gun."

Ella's eyebrows jumped, and her mouth flattened, as though she was barely holding in her disgust.

"Sean," Logan said sharply, and the man dropped Ella's hand. Finally. "We have a few questions for you."

Sean nodded, smoothed a hand over his wrinkled shirt. "Sure. You're wondering about the girl who went missing a few days ago, right?

The one whose friend was on the news last night? You want to know if I saw anyone sniffing around her at the bars?"

"Well—" Logan began.

"Yes," Ella cut him off. "What can you tell us about that?"

Sean stepped a little closer. "I saw her at one of the bars. She was dancing with every guy in the room."

"Did she dance with you?"

Sean's head jerked back, then he looked Ella up and down. "No way. I like them a little older."

"What about Theresa Crowley? Did you see her anywhere?"

"The one who was found in the marsh?" Sean glanced at Logan, then back at Ella, and his tone was cooler as he answered, "Sure, I saw her around town with Logan's sister. Never talked to her, though. Like I said, I like my women a little older than that. Is that all? I've got places to be."

Probably another bar, Logan thought. "Just one more question. It's about your van." He paused, watching Sean's reaction carefully.

Sean looked at Ella, then down at the ground, then back at Logan. "What about it?"

"You let anyone else drive it?"

"No. Not really."

"Which one?"

Sean seemed confused. "Which one what?"

Logan held in a sigh. "No or not really?"

"Usually not. But sometimes, if I have too many beers, I'll let one of my friends drive."

"You ever let anyone borrow the van?"

"Nah."

Logan stepped closer, invaded Sean's space. "Have you been to the Traveler's Hotel recently?" It was the hotel where Ella had been followed by a blue van.

Sean backed up. "No."

"Are you sure?"

"Yeah, I'm sure," Sean barked. "You got anything else you want to ask me? 'Cause I'm getting sick of this."

Logan locked a steady glare on Sean until he took another step back. "Nope, that's it."

As Sean spun and headed back the way he'd come, Logan called, "Stay away from the hotels, Sean."

"What was that about?" Ella asked as they got back into his car.

"You don't think he could have been the one following you at your hotel?"

Ella studied Sean, watching him out the window. "Maybe."

Logan shifted into drive, going back to the station, frustrated. He was glad Ella was at a different hotel from the one where she'd been followed, but he didn't like that she was now across town from the police station. If he thought there was any chance of talking her into staying with him, he would have tried. But he knew she'd refuse, so instead he said, "I know

Sean's not socially awkward, but how do you like him for a killer?"

Ella was silent for so long that Logan glanced over at her.

"Well, I guess *socially awkward* isn't the word for what he is. I was just going to call him *creepy*. Do women fall for that?"

Logan shrugged. "Spring breakers at the bars? I think they do."

"Ew."

A smile hitched his lips, then faded. "Well? What do you think?"

"I'm not sure, Logan. Sean is predatory, but he doesn't really fit the profile. *I* may find him awkward." There was irritation in her tone as she added, "I mean, why did he keep talking about liking older women as though that was supposed to be charming? Women don't like anyone to talk about their age."

"Yeah, well, all his talk about liking women out of college is nonsense anyway. Why do you think he's not working during spring break?"

"You're kidding me. He takes off work to hit on college students?"

"Yep."

Ella's nose wrinkled with distaste. "Well, he definitely came off as slimy. And I'm not crazy about the fact that he specifically mentioned seeing Theresa around with Becky."

Logan's head whipped toward her, then back to the road, his hands tightening around the wheel. "You think he was watching them?"

"I think he noticed them. Enough that he knew exactly who you meant. But like I said, he doesn't fit the profile. He may be creepy, but *he* doesn't think he's awkward at all. He wouldn't feel compelled to lure anyone out to a secluded location to grab them. He's more sure of himself than that. He'd take them right home from the bar." She compressed her lips, as if she was considering, then shook her head. "We should keep an eye on him, but I don't think he's the killer."

Logan's hands relaxed. "Okay. What about the other interviews?"

"Well, Joe definitely doesn't fit. His social skills aren't there, but he was pretty forthcoming about everything. And he showed no interest in the investigation or concern about the questioning. As for Adam's nephew or his shrimping crew? I don't know. Adam was lying about the van, but I kind of doubt he knows whether someone who works for him is a killer and he's covering for that person."

Logan's frustration grew, the frustration he'd been feeling ever since Theresa's body had turned up and he'd had no idea where to look. All along, his gut had told him it was a serial killer who was so good at it that he'd managed to avoid detection until now.

Maybe the killer was so good he was never going to be caught.

Chapter Twelve

When Logan pulled his Chevy Caprice into the station lot, the first thing Ella noticed was Lyla Evans sitting on the front steps, no camera crew in sight.

As soon as Lyla spotted them, she stood and crossed her arms over her chest. She walked toward them like a woman on a mission. Even from a distance, she looked royally pissed off.

"Uh-oh," Ella said.

Logan cursed. "She probably heard that I questioned Joe."

"I guess now isn't a good time to ask her to lay off the FBI references in her newscasts." Ella said, only half-joking.

Logan's eyes darted upward and he made a noise somewhere between amusement and frustration. "Somebody save me from strong-willed women."

Ella gave him a look of disbelief, and he mumbled, "Or from myself."

As Lyla neared Logan's car, he said, "Why don't you go inside? I'll meet you in there." He took the keys from the ignition. "I have a feeling this might get ugly."

"Are you sure—"

"Yes. If I don't join you in ten minutes, send out a rescue party, okay?"

Ella laughed. "You need rescuing from the supermodel?"

Logan's forehead furrowed and Ella instantly regretted her smart-aleck response—and letting him know Lyla's looks intimidated her. "I'll meet you inside," she blurted, then hopped out of the car.

Outside, Lyla glared at her, pretty features twisted in an ugly snarl, but she quickly redirected her anger at Logan when he stepped out of the Chevy Caprice, too.

Ella considered saying something, but figured she'd only make it worse. So, instead, she speed-walked toward the station.

Behind her, she heard Lyla demand, "You questioned my brother about a *serial killer* case like he was some kind of suspect? How dare you!"

"Lyla," Logan said, "Just because I know Joe doesn't mean I can—"

"Was this *her* idea?" Lyla spat.

"Look, we were running down a lead," Logan said calmly. "If I only question people I don't know, it would compromise the investigation."

"A lead," Lyla replied, then her voice faded as Ella got farther away. But she got loud again. "Just because you have a crush on the profiler and want to impress her—"

Ella stumbled. She quickly righted herself, hoping Logan hadn't noticed, especially as he cut Lyla off loudly enough for Ella to hear.

"She's in town for the case, Lyla. And she lives in Virginia." There was such finality in his voice, as though there was no real chance for a relationship between them, and it should have been obvious.

Ella wrenched open the door to the station. Before it closed behind her, she heard Lyla say, "Yeah, believe me, I know that no one's an option unless she lives right here in Oakville."

The venom in Lyla's voice surprised Ella. Why had Logan and Lyla broken up? She knew Lyla had moved somewhere else in Florida, but it couldn't have been that far if she was here now, reporting on the serial killer story. Had Logan really been unwilling to compromise even that much?

If he hadn't, then Scott was wrong. Long-distance with Logan wasn't an option.

An ache formed in Ella's chest and she pressed a hand to it, trying to will it away. Sure, she'd had strong hopes for starting something with

Logan, something real. But she'd only known him for...

Ella's steps faltered. She'd only known him for six days. It felt like so much longer. In some ways, it felt as if she had known him all her life, which made no sense.

As much as she'd hoped to jump into a serious relationship with Logan, maybe she'd been fooling herself. People didn't form attachments this fast. Not attachments that lasted anyway. It wasn't logical.

"How's the case going?"

Ella blinked and looked up, realizing she'd stopped just inside the station. Hank was standing in front of her, holding open the door into the locked area.

"Uh, thanks." Ella stepped into the part of the station reserved for police officers, where she'd been working with Logan over the past week. "The case is going slowly." She frowned, thinking about all the contradictory evidence they had. "This killer is smart. Very smart."

Hank nodded. He actually patted her on the back with his enormous hand as he said, "I have faith. Logan said you're the key. He said that if we really do have a serial killer, you'll be the one to figure out who it is."

He had? A new tension tightened her chest— the pressure to figure out something she was starting to worry she no longer knew how to do. "I hope so," she said faintly.

Hank looked at her oddly, maybe because he was used to her being a lot more aggressive and confident. "Well, let me know if I can help." He headed out the door.

"Thanks," she called after him belatedly, then took a fortifying breath and hurried into the conference room. Now was not the time to be having doubts.

Every killer left behind clues, no matter how hard he tried to disguise them. This one was no different. And with Logan's help, she *knew* they could find him. She refused to accept any other possibility.

That decided, she got a coffee and settled at the conference table to wait for Logan.

She didn't have to wait long. He pushed open the door and told her, "Lyla's going to stop mentioning the FBI."

"Really?" That was the last thing she'd expected him to say. "Wow, you must be persuasive."

Logan poured himself a cup of coffee, downed half of it, then sat next to her. "Hardly. Apparently whatever you said to her the other night made an impression. She wants to coordinate with the station on future stories to help us catch this guy. She wasn't happy about us questioning her brother, but she seems sincere about this."

"Seriously?"

"Yeah, seriously. She yelled at me for five minutes about us talking to Joe, and then she calmed down and said she wants to work with us." He gave her a half grin. "So, apparently, *you're* the persuasive one."

He took another sip of coffee, then added,

"Which doesn't surprise me. You could persuade me into just about anything."

If only that were true.

Ella forced a brief smile, then got down to business. "I feel we're missing something that should be obvious. I think we should analyze what we've got again, see if it sparks any new ideas."

Logan was looking at her quizzically, as if he knew she was considering some thought she hadn't divulged, so she picked up the pad on the table and started jotting notes. "We know Theresa stayed in town past her scheduled departure. We *think* she told the woman at the gas station that she was meeting someone at your grandparents' house, but it's possible either the woman or Theresa was lying."

Logan leaned in close as he braced his arms on the table, looking over her notes. "Why would the witness lie?"

"I have no idea. The killer works alone, so

unless this woman knows who it is and is trying to protect him—"

"I doubt it," Logan said. "She's in her late seventies and she was my grandma's friend. I mean, she does have grandkids in their twenties, but I have a hard time believing she'd make up this story to cover for one of them. Besides, if she was going to lie, why lie about my grandparents' house? It's not like I was the one questioning her. And even if I was, how would that help?"

Ella agreed with him, but she wanted to separate what they knew for sure from what they only believed. "What about Theresa? Maybe she was lying, either about where she was going, or why."

Logan nodded slowly. "Well, we didn't see any evidence she was at the house, so maybe that's not where she was going. But that doesn't explain why she was still in town."

"I know." Ella frowned at her meager notes.

"And that has to be the key. Why was she still here?"

"Her cell phone records seemed like a bust," Logan reminded her. "There were no calls besides Becky's after Theresa left for the airport. Maybe this guy really did run into her along the way and then convinced her to stay, but to drive separately to meet him somewhere." Logan shrugged. "Maybe he told her he needed to make a stop first and he'd meet her there? And I still have no clue *who* she'd possibly stay for."

"Okay. What about Laurie? Were the officers able to track down where she went after she left that guy's house? The one who picked her up at the bar?"

Logan shook his head. "Jeff told us that when she left, she planned to go back to wherever her friend Kelly was. And Kelly says she was at the hotel, so we can assume Laurie was heading there. Probably she ran into this guy along the way. But we haven't come up with any witnesses who saw her after she left Jeff's place."

Logan lifted his coffee, but then set it back down. "What about the killer? I know we've been assuming all along it was a man. I thought that from the beginning, because I suspected sexual assault, but the autopsy didn't come up with anything. The damage from the marsh and the alligator was too extreme to say for sure. Could I have been wrong? Could we be looking for a woman?"

This time Ella shook her head. "It's unlikely. Even without sexual assault—and I actually wouldn't be surprised to learn there was none— the behavioral details suggest a man. Is it within the realm of possibility that it's a woman? Yes. But my professional opinion is that we're looking for a man, and I suspect he's somewhere between twenty and forty."

Logan nodded and gulped down the rest of his coffee.

"Actually, maybe we need to think more about

the burns." She knew Logan wasn't going to like this, given that he'd known the victim, but the burns were important. "Even though we've determined Theresa's injuries weren't branding, the burns could still tell us something about the killer."

"Okay. You mentioned before that it could be how he tortures, right? If he's a sadist?" Logan's words were a little strangled, but he wasn't backing away from the topic.

Ella put a hand over his, knowing this had to be a hard subject, and Logan turned his hand over and fit his fingers between hers.

Ella stared down at their linked hands, holding on a little tighter as if it would keep Logan connected to her.

Focus, Cortez.

"Yes. And serial arsonists and serial killers often share a desire to control, so that could be part of the appeal of fire for this guy. If inflicting pain to get a response from the victim is his end goal, then fire could simply be his means.

But there's a very good chance that fire has some special significance to him."

"Right. You said maybe the killer had burns himself?"

"Yes, and if he does, they would be severe."

Logan frowned. "I don't know anyone like that. And I'm not sure how we'd get that information, other than maybe just asking around."

"Maybe we should call the fire stations, here and in the neighboring towns, see if they can give us any insight."

"Sure, let's try," Logan said, but he sounded as discouraged as she felt.

Who was this killer? Usually, by this point, Ella would have been firmly in his head. She would've been able to anticipate his next move, and she'd have a much clearer picture of what kind of person he was, and why he killed.

Usually, she also had more to go on. More victims, more crime scenes, just more. But still, her instincts were humming, persistently telling her that she was missing something important.

Ella knew if she didn't figure out what that was, the killer was going to get away with murdering Theresa. And right now, he was probably already targeting someone else, maybe even Logan's little sister.

She couldn't let that happen.

"I COULD REALLY use a few rounds with a punching bag right about now," Ella told Logan as she buckled up.

They'd spent the rest of the day talking to the different fire stations, tracking down information on burn victims in Oakville and the neighboring towns. But all of the leads had fizzled fast.

They were one day closer to Ella needing to leave, and she felt no closer to the killer's identity. Frustration boiled inside of her, with no ready outlet.

"Me, too," Logan said as he started up the car. "I've got one in my basement. You're welcome to come over and work out your aggression there."

Ella studied his profile as he pulled away from the station to drive her back to her hotel. She stared at the hard lines of his face, which looked formidable, until he smiled. And then he'd flash those green eyes at her and all her brain cells would cease to function until the only thing left was a powerful yearning.

Wanting to be with someone had never been so complicated for her before. Usually, if she was interested, she gave it a shot. Usually, everything was light and easy and simple until it was over. And she might be sad for a while, might be perplexed about what had gone wrong, but she'd never felt this much angst over anyone. Never felt this soul-deep certainty that to lose this man might be more than she could bear.

Every time she looked at Logan, she was tempted to take what she could get, while she was here, but then her brain would shout a warning that it wouldn't be enough. And if she wanted anything more, she was going to have to take a risk.

So she swallowed her fear, took a deep breath, and asked the question she'd been wondering for days. "Why did you and Lyla break up?"

At her quiet, serious tone, Logan glanced at her. The car slowed before he seemed to realize what he was doing and he put his foot back down on the gas. "I thought we might get onto this topic again."

Her immediate instinct was to backtrack, to tell him he didn't have to answer if he didn't want to, but instead she kept her mouth shut and waited. Her heart pounded as she hoped he'd tell her it was about more than just the distance. Because if he wouldn't leave Oakville for a fiancée, what chance was there for some woman who'd known him less than a week?

And for her, there was no option besides Aquia. She couldn't be an FBI profiler anywhere else. And she'd changed the entire course of her life, become estranged from her family, worked way too many hours, to get there. Now she was finally in a job where she might actually be able to bring down the Fishhook Rapist, fulfill the unspoken part of her pact with Scott and Maggie from a decade ago.

"Around the time my promotion to detective came through, Lyla got the offer for the position as an on-camera reporter. I knew that's what she wanted to do and Oakville doesn't have a local news affiliate."

Logan watched the road, his forehead creased as he continued. "In the end, that's what did it. She wanted to go and I wanted to stay. Finally, we agreed it wasn't going to work. My whole family is here, and you can probably tell we're really close. I never planned to leave Oakville. I thought she'd be happy here, too."

He lifted his shoulders. "I guess it's probably good she got the offer when she did and not after we were married, because our relationship wasn't strong enough to make it through that."

Ella nodded, as though she understood, but

she really didn't. How could they not work through something like that? It wasn't as though Lyla had left Florida, so Logan would still have been close to his family. And he could have been a detective anywhere.

But then again, she'd never been in a relationship where she'd even considered something as serious as marriage, so who was she to say? Because if it came right down to it, she didn't know if she could ever leave Aquia, leave BAU, even after they found the Fishhook Rapist. Not for any guy. Not even someone she wanted as desperately as she wanted Logan.

Logan glanced at her, as though waiting for her to comment, but what was there to say? If another city in Florida was too far from his family, Virginia was out of the question. Yeah, maybe short-term they could make long-distance work, but where would that ultimately leave them? If they didn't have a shot at a real future, why set herself up for heartbreak? So, she just nodded again, looking out the window even though it was too dark to see anything but the headlights from other cars.

When he pulled up in front of her hotel and put the car in park, she turned toward him. She couldn't seem to smile, couldn't seem to bring herself to say anything at all, so she just unhooked her seatbelt, leaned into him and pressed her lips to his.

Whenever she'd kissed him in the past, it had been almost instantaneous combustion. But this time, his hand slid around to the back of her head, and he kissed her slowly, thoroughly. The scruff on his chin scratched as his lips caressed hers softly, over and over. It was as if he was giving her a chance to memorize the feel of him. As if he knew it would be the last time.

When he finally pulled back, Ella blinked rapidly, trying to keep the moisture in her eyes at bay, then got out of his car before she could change her mind and beg him to come with her. Beg him never to leave.

Knowing she'd made the right choice didn't

stop the tears from spilling over as she went into the hotel alone. And it didn't stop a heavy weight from pressing on her chest, as though she'd just lost something very, very important.

"LOGAN?"

Ella sat up in bed, his name on her lips before she was fully conscious, before she even realized what had awakened her. She blinked at the alarm clock next to her bed. 6:00 a.m.

Then she stretched across the bed to grab her ringing phone. "Isabella Cortez," she said, her voice still husky with sleep.

"Ella, it's Logan."

Come over. The words were already forming on her lips when Logan spoke.

"We found Laurie Donaldson."

Dread rushed through Ella at Logan's dire tone, and she was instantly wide-awake.

"She was in the marsh. There's no question now, Ella. We were right. We've got a serial killer."

And if he'd dumped Laurie's body, he would soon be trolling for a new victim.

Ella pushed back the covers. "I'm on my way."

Chapter Thirteen

Everyone in Oakville was frantic and afraid. Locals and tourists alike were crammed into every available space in the front area of the police station, demanding answers.

Logan kept his head down and pushed through them to the locked door and into the back room. But everyone in town knew he was lead on the case, and the questions followed him.

How close were the police to finding the killer? How were they supposed to keep themselves safe? How could this happen in Oakville, of all places?

Logan didn't have any good answers, so he didn't even try to respond. He just pulled the door closed behind him and rubbed a hand over his eyes, which felt like sandpaper after only five hours of sleep.

As soon as the call had come in, he'd thrown on the first clothes he'd found in his closet and raced to the morgue, where Laurie's body had just been taken. He'd stayed for the autopsy, then called Ella on his way to the station.

He'd wanted to call her as soon as he got the news. He'd had his cell phone in hand, her number already dialed, when he'd changed his mind. As a detective, he'd stood through autopsies before. Every single time, he'd puked his guts out as soon as he left. This time had been no different.

But Logan knew Ella, as a profiler, wouldn't normally go to the autopsies. She dealt with the aftermath, and that was bad enough.

He knew she'd insist on being there if he called her, so he'd waited, hoping to spare her from having those images burned into her brain.

Logan pressed a hand to his mouth, trying not

to gag as one of the images he'd had imprinted in his mind rushed forward. He didn't think anything was going to be as bad as witnessing Theresa's autopsy, since he'd known her when she was alive. But the knowledge that he'd been chasing this killer when Laurie was grabbed, the knowledge that he could have prevented it if he'd found the killer, had made this autopsy just as difficult.

Logan entered the conference room, and the smell of burnt coffee wafting up from the carafe made his stomach churn, even though there couldn't possibly have been anything left in there.

"Logan." Hank clapped a hand on his arm. "You were right." There was newfound respect in Hank's voice as he shook his head and said, "It really is a serial killer."

Logan looked up from the T-shirt he just noticed he'd put on backward in his haste to get moving when he'd gotten the call. "I wish I hadn't been."

"I hear you."

"Wait. Where's Ella?" He'd sent Hank to pick her up, not wanting Ella to walk all the way to the station from the other side of Oakville. Not alone. Not with a serial killer loose. He didn't care how many people were around at this time of day. "She was waiting at the hotel for you, wasn't she?"

Logan heard the panic in his voice and Hank must have, too, because he said, "Relax. She's right behind me."

And when Hank moved aside, there was Ella. Relief rushed through Logan.

Instead of her usual knee-length skirt and T-shirt loose enough to hide her holster, Ella was wearing a pair of capris and a tank top, her gun on display on her hip. Her hair was tied back in a messy ponytail and dark circles showed below her eyes. But she was unhurt, and so, to him, she looked perfect.

Her expression was grim. "Who found Laurie's body?"

Logan gave himself a second to absorb the fact that Ella really was okay, then said, "A couple of tourists who decided they wanted to kayak deep into the marsh and watch the sunrise from there. Luckily, one of them took a cell phone and they called us when they spotted her. Officers on duty borrowed a boat and went out to get her. I just got back from the autopsy."

Ella paused midway to the table, blinking at him. She sounded a little hurt when she asked, "Why didn't you call me earlier?"

Hank took that as his cue to leave, backing out of the room quickly.

"I didn't think there was any reason for both of us to have to watch that," Logan said. Trying to lighten the mood, he added, "Plus, I figured you might think less of me if I threw up on your shoes."

"Thanks. I've never had to watch an autopsy." She crossed her arms, as if the very idea gave her chills. "The photos are hard enough."

He nodded at the folder he'd put on the table

as he sat down. "I'm afraid I brought some of those. I thought you might want to see them, in case it tells you something about the killer."

Ella was still for a moment, then her shoulders stiffened and she marched to the table and sat beside him, fast, as if she didn't want to give herself time to change her mind. Whether it was about seeing the photos or getting close to him, he wasn't entirely sure.

When she was next to him, he wanted to wrap his hand around hers—to comfort himself as much as her. If it had been yesterday, he would have. But that kiss she'd given him last night…

It had felt like goodbye.

He'd known she wouldn't like hearing the reason his last serious relationship hadn't worked. That he'd thought enough of someone to propose marriage, but hadn't stuck by his promise. But at least he and Lyla had both realized it would be a mistake before going through with it. And he'd told Ella the truth. He wasn't going to lie to her.

But where did that leave them? With her returning home in a week at the very most? Especially now, when she'd obviously made the decision to resist this pull between them. How was he going to breach her defenses? *Could* he breach them?

He was an idiot. He was an idiot for getting drawn into the discussion about Lyla. He was an idiot for falling for Ella in the first place. Because what he'd told Lyla was true—Ella lived too far away.

And both of them had jobs that demanded all their time. It wasn't as if the investigations would stop coming just because it was a weekend. Ella's job was probably worse. Even if they *did* try to make something long-distance happen, how long before visits started getting cancelled because of cases? Too much of that and a relationship would fizzle, no matter how much he wanted it.

What chance did they have, really?

But as he looked at her now, her dark brown

eyes so serious and wary as she stared back at him, he knew he had to try. Because as much of an idiot as it made him, he loved her.

It was ridiculous. He knew that. He'd met her fewer than two weeks ago; genuine love shouldn't have been able to develop that fast. But he didn't doubt that was what he felt. It was too intense, too tied up in things that went way beyond simple lust.

So, instead of denying himself what he could have in their short time together, he took her hand tightly in his. He locked his eyes on hers, wondering if her intuitive profiler mind could read exactly what he was feeling.

Her lips parted and he thought she was going to say something, but then she ducked her head and pulled her hand free. "We'd better get started," she said, but her voice was barely above a whisper.

Dismay filled him, but he forced himself to focus. Laurie might have been past saving, but she deserved justice. And she deserved his full attention.

He pulled the folder closer for Ella. "We only recovered a partial body, because of the alligators, but Laurie's body was dumped a few days ago. And she was burned, same as Theresa." His voice caught and he cleared his throat. Was this ever going to get any easier?

"A few days ago? I thought officers checked the marsh when she originally went missing."

"They did. But she wasn't found in the same area as Theresa and we have a large system of marshes here."

Ella nodded and opened the folder containing the autopsy photos. "There are a lot more burns this time."

She looked up, staring vacantly ahead of her as she let out a long breath. "It doesn't matter how much of this kind of thing I see, every time, *every time*, it boggles my mind how one person can do this to another."

She clutched the edge of the table and he

resisted the urge to reach for her hand again, knowing she'd pull away.

"I mean, I can get into the killers' heads, deconstruct them on a psychological level. Abusive home life, lack of empathy, need for control, whatever." Her voice picked up speed, picked up fury. "But at the end of the day, I'm just left wondering *why.*"

She closed her eyes and he could see her trying to regain composure. He expected her to open them again and go back to the folder, go back to her clinical profiler voice and tell him whatever else she could about this killer.

Instead, when she opened her eyes and turned to look directly into his, he saw tears brimming there. "After we made that pact—Maggie, Scott and I—I wanted this job with the FBI, this particular role at BAU, because I wanted to understand. Like maybe that would, I don't know, make some kind of sense of it all. Make some kind of sense of what had happened to Maggie."

A tear rolled down her cheek and Logan felt

her hurt as an ache in his own chest. Not caring if she rebuffed him again, he took her hand in one of his and wiped the tear away with the other.

This time, she didn't pull away. She squeezed his hand tighter as she told him, "It doesn't. None of it makes any sense." He could feel her shaking as she said, "But usually, I'm good at this. And being able to get into the killer's head means fewer victims. That's why I stay. Because I feel like it matters."

She looked at the folder again, then shook her head. "Days like these, though, and I wonder what I'm doing."

She released a loud breath that sounded almost like a laugh. "Sorry. That was morose." She turned on her tough profiler voice. "I can do this. Let's go over the details and catch this guy."

Logan kept hold of her hand, rubbed his thumb over her knuckles. "I know you can. And

I admire you even more because it's hard for you and you do it anyway."

Ella turned to him, her eyes unreadable as she studied him for a long moment. "You always know the right thing to say to make me feel better," she finally said softly. "No wonder you're so hard to resist."

"THERE'S NO QUESTION we have a serial killer in Oakville."

Police Chief Patterson made that announcement from a podium at the front of the briefing room, which was filled with officers from every shift. Most of them looked exhausted from pulling relentless overtime, and grim from the recent discovery of Laurie's body.

"Until now, the serial killer angle was considered a remote possibility," the chief continued and Ella glanced at Logan, sitting next to her.

Weariness showed in every line of his face, in the droop of his eyelids, and the longer-than-usual stubble on his chin. But beneath it, Ella still saw the simmering anger over what had been done to the victims, and the relentless determination that had driven him to fight his chief every step of the way to let him chase his serial killer theory.

"But Detective Greer was convinced enough about this to bring in an FBI profiler. And he was right."

Surprise flashed briefly across Logan's features. He'd probably never expected the chief to say those words.

Ella's hand twitched, wanting to reach for Logan's. He deserved the recognition. He was a dedicated and talented detective, and it was about time Oakville realized how lucky they were to have him.

She was biased. She knew it. But the truth was, she'd coordinated with a lot of detectives in her work at the BAU, and Logan *was* exceptionally good. How many other detectives would have seen Theresa's case and recognized a potential serial killer? Heck, even her boss had turned the case down, which meant he hadn't seen it. And he'd been dealing with serial killers his entire career.

"The FBI profiler is going to talk to us now, tell us new details about this killer to help us nail him," Chief Patterson continued, refocusing Ella's attention.

She wished he'd remembered to remind everyone that her consultation was unofficial, that the officers were supposed to keep any discussion of her involvement entirely in-station.

Her boss at the BAU knew she was here, but he'd told her in no uncertain terms that the trip hadn't been approved. She might be sure they had a serial killer on their hands, but it still wasn't an FBI case because it hadn't been through the proper channels.

But hopefully they'd find the killer soon and it wouldn't become an issue. Ella stood and took her place behind the podium, wishing she'd taken the time to put on something more businesslike. "Most of you know me by now. But for those of you who don't, I'm Ella Cortez. I work for the FBI's Behavioral Analysis Unit, creating profiles of killers like this one. I'm here on my own time, but I've been working with Lo—Detective Greer over the past week and we have some points we'd like to go over today."

She looked down at the list she'd jotted, which was still pitifully short. But it was better than nothing.

Scanning the room, she said, "This killer has a type. If you haven't already, look at the pictures of the victims. They're both college age with long, dark hair. And when they were abducted, they were both supposedly leaving town. We're working now to coordinate a piece with the local news warning women to be particularly careful as they leave town to head home."

Lyla was going to do the story on tonight's eleven o'clock news. They'd talked to her earlier in the day. It had been awkward, but when it was over, Ella'd had to admit that maybe she'd misjudged Lyla. And from the way Lyla had been looking at Logan during most of the meeting, she had a feeling Lyla was having second thoughts about their breakup.

A sour feeling climbed up Ella's throat, but she tried to ignore it. As much as she might want a claim on Logan, she didn't have one.

She continued, "The killer is a loner, unmarried, between the ages of twenty and forty. He's socially awkward. We still don't know how he's luring his victims, but before he kills them, he's burning them. And there's a very good chance that the killer has scars from burns himself. If you know of anyone like that in the area, talk to Detective Greer right away. Otherwise, we need to look for someone who has these kinds of scars. But we need to do it quietly and carefully. Because if the killer thinks we're getting too close, he might take drastic measures, including grabbing more victims."

The officers in the room all stared back at her, listening intently.

"There's one final thing. It's possible the killer

is using a dark blue van in the commission of these crimes. Any potential suspect with access to that type of vehicle should be approached with particular care."

When Ella stepped away from the podium, the officers looked around, as if they'd been expecting more. As if they'd been expecting her to hand them a miracle. She could only regret her inability to do it.

"That's all," Chief Patterson said. "For everyone who's not on shift right now, thanks for coming in. For those of you who are, get back out there."

As the officers slowly filed out of the room, Ella looked at Logan. Finding Laurie's body had confirmed the things they'd suspected. But it hadn't really told them anything new about this killer.

On Logan's face, she saw reflected the same thing she was thinking—did they know enough? Could they find him before he claimed another victim?

ELLA HAD JUST turned on the TV to watch the live segment on the news when her cell phone rang. She glanced at it across the room and debated ignoring it. It wasn't Logan calling, because he and Chief Patterson were about to be interviewed live by Lyla. But it could still be about the case, so she hit mute and stood up.

Hopefully, it was one of Adam Pawlter's shrimping crew returning her calls. She and Logan had tried to catch them after she'd given her profile at the station, but they'd gone back out on the boat. She would have rather talked to them in person, but over the phone was better than nothing.

She answered the phone just as it was about to go to voice mail. "Isabella Cortez."

"Hi, there. Ella's short for Isabella, is it? I like that."

The voice was a man's and it instantly gave her the creeps, but Ella didn't recognize it. She tried to focus as an image of Lyla inside the police station appeared on the TV screen. "Who's speaking?"

"This is Sean. Sean Fink. We met yesterday near my house, remember?"

Ah, that explained the slime practically oozing through the phone. "Mr. Fink. How did you get my number?"

Sean sounded proud of himself as he replied, "I got it from someone at the station. I told them I had some information you wanted."

Unbelievable. Ella tried to keep her tone neutral as she watched Logan and Chief Patterson come on-screen for the interview. "What information is that?"

"Well, I was thinking some more about what you asked me the other day. About seeing Theresa and Laurie around town before they went missing? I realized I had some more details that could help you."

As soon as Sean mentioned the victims by name, Ella's attention was entirely on the phone call. When they'd talked to him yesterday, he'd referred to Laurie as simply the girl who'd gone missing. He would likely have seen her name in the news, but the casual way he'd just thrown out their names, as if he'd known them all along, had the hair on the back of Ella's neck standing at attention.

She wanted to talk to Adam's nephew and the others in the shrimping crew primarily because of the blue van that had seemed to set Adam on edge. But Sean Fink had a blue van, too.

She clicked the TV off and asked, "What can you tell me?"

"I thought we should meet," Sean said. "I'm at your hotel now."

Chills danced down Ella's spine and she fought to keep the suspicion out of her voice. "I wasn't aware that you knew where I was staying."

Sean laughed and Ella realized he was at least a little bit drunk. "It was pretty obvious from what Logan said yesterday. I'm at the Traveler's Hotel."

The nerves clutching Ella's stomach relaxed. At least he wasn't here. But the Traveler's Hotel was where she'd been followed by the blue van.

She'd dismissed Sean from her suspect list, thinking he was too sure of himself to be the killer, but she might have been wrong. Maybe the persona of confident, smarmy flirt was brought on by alcohol. Maybe when he wasn't drinking, he was awkward and socially inept. Maybe he was a killer.

Ella reached for her gun. "Sure, I'll meet you. But how about we do it at the coffee shop near the police station? Say twenty minutes?"

The coffee shop was open twenty-four hours and catered mostly to cops and tourists. It was closer to the Traveler's Hotel than where she was staying now. Without a car, it would take her fifteen minutes to get there. That gave her five to change out of her pajamas and call Logan.

There was a pause. "Yeah, okay, I guess that'll work. I'll see you soon."

As Sean hung up, Ella tried not to imagine

anything ominous in his last words. There was a chance he was the killer, yes, but more likely he was just clueless, intoxicated and trying to use the case to hit on her again.

But as Ella threw on a pair of jeans and a T-shirt, she had to wonder. What if he trolled for victims and set up meetings with them when he was drunk and full of liquid courage? Sober, and back to feeling awkward and shy, he might want the women somewhere isolated to grab them. And he certainly knew the area well enough to use the marshes as disposal sites.

As Ella left her hotel room, she called Logan. But her call went directly to voice mail, and when she looked at her watch, she realized he was probably still on air. She left him a message as she ran down the stairs instead of bothering with the elevator.

Outside, the air was crisp and just cool enough that she wished she had a jacket. And dark enough that she wished she'd brought her flashlight. But once she jogged down the long entryway to the hotel, she'd be on the main street through town, which was usually lit up until the bars closed.

Could Sean actually have legitimate information? Or was she letting her nerves get the better of her?

Shaking her head at herself, Ella jogged around the corner. If nothing else, this was a good excuse to work off some extra energy. She had plenty, between the frustrating hours of investigating and the tension of another sort that buzzed through her whenever she came within five feet of Logan.

Ella increased her pace, her pulse spiking after a week of having her butt planted in a chair or driving around with Logan running down leads. In the distance, she heard cars and people on the main strip.

And what was that rumbling? Ella wondered as she rounded another corner.

As soon as she did, a dark blue van picked up speed, veering quickly toward her.

Ella reached instantly for her gun, but the car was coming too fast, its headlights blinding her. Panic rose in her chest as Ella saw that there was nowhere to go. Into the street was a bad option and there was a steep embankment on her other side. She whipped her gun free of its holster, squeezed off two shots and jumped to the left anyway.

She flew through the air, momentarily weightless and suspended, then gravity took hold and she slammed into the packed dirt, landing hard on her shoulder and hip. Her head bounced off the ground, and then she was rolling, faster and faster, down the side of the embankment.

Branches tore at her arms, something whacked her forehead, and Ella tried to grab at anything to stop her fall. When she finally hit the rise on the bottom, her whole body felt bruised. She blinked and tried to push herself up, but the world spun and she dropped back down.

Above her, a car revved its engine and Ella

reached for her gun once more. But she'd lost it during her fall.

She sucked in a deep breath, and grasped the nearest sturdy stick she might be able to use as a weapon. Then she crawled farther into the shadows, still trying to get her equilibrium and her vision back.

Above her, a light suddenly shone down and then someone came pounding down the embankment.

Ella raised the stick over her head.

Chapter Fourteen

"Shots fired at the Oceanview Lodge."

The call came over dispatch as Logan was walking out of the conference room at the station, Chief Patterson on his heels.

Next to him, Lyla was saying something about how well the story had gone, about how maybe they should go get some coffee and talk.

Fear instantly rose up and Logan grabbed Hank's sleeve as he hurried past. "Did I hear that right?"

"Oceanview Lodge," Hank said. "Shots fired." He paused and glanced back at Logan, realization on his face. "Ella's hotel. Come on. You can hitch a ride with us."

Ignoring whatever Lyla was saying, Logan started to run.

What had he been thinking, simply moving Ella to another hotel after the blue van had followed her? It wasn't as if Oakville had dozens of hotels. It wouldn't have been hard for a motivated killer to track her down. He should have insisted she stay with him, insisted on having eyes on her at all times.

Instead, she was on the other side of town. It would only take a few minutes to get there, the way Hank drove, but with a gun in the mix, that was way too long.

He jumped into the transport section of Hank's police cruiser and slapped the back of Hank's seat. "Go!"

As soon as Hank's partner got into the passenger seat, Hank peeled out fast enough to make Logan's head slam back against the headrest. *Faster*, Logan wanted to say, but there was traffic and, even at nearly midnight, pedestrians. The drive to the hotel took fewer than five minutes, but by the time they got there, Logan was shaky with fear.

The drive leading up to the hotel was lit up with the headlights of two police cruisers that had gotten there before them. Sitting in the glow of the lights, just inside an open ambulance, was Ella.

Relief hit hard and fast, but the fear didn't go away entirely. Ella was holding a compress to her head while an EMT bent over her arm.

Hank jerked to a stop and Logan tried to get out, but couldn't, since he was behind the cage. It only took a few seconds for Hank to open the door and let him out, but it was long enough for Logan to realize just how unnaturally fast his heart was going.

He'd been to a lot of crime scenes in his career as a police officer. He'd never felt this terrified.

He jumped out of the cruiser. "Ella!"

"Logan." She sounded relieved that he'd arrived. Or maybe that was just his wishful thinking.

He hurried to her side and by the time he got there, he'd already noted every scrape and bruise along her bare arms, the nasty bump on her head, and the angry, jagged slash in her T-shirt. "Is she okay?" he asked the EMT.

"She'll be fine." The EMT frowned at Ella as he told Logan, "I'd prefer she go to the hospital and get this one stitched up." He gestured to the gash on her arm that he was working on. "But she says she didn't lose consciousness, and it doesn't look like she has a concussion. It can't feel good, but she'll be okay."

Logan's heart rate slowed down a notch. His arms were tensed with the need to hold her, but he forced himself to stay still and let the EMT fix her up. "What happened? We got a call of shots fired."

Ella looked up at him, and in her eyes he could see pain and residual fear.

The desire to wrap his arms around her intensified until he didn't care that he was going to annoy the EMT, didn't care who was watching. He climbed up into the ambulance on the other side of Ella and carefully placed an arm around her waist. "Are you okay?"

"She was okay enough to nearly beat the crap out of me with a stick when I went to help her," their rookie officer piped up.

Next to him, Ella grimaced. "Sorry about that. You were shining your flashlight into my eyes. I couldn't tell you were police."

The rookie's partner laughed as he trudged up next to them. "We heard the shots and put the call out over the radio," he told Logan. "We identified ourselves, but I guess not loud enough." He handed Ella a weapon. "We found your gun down there."

"Thanks."

As the officer walked away, he added, amusement in his voice, "We've learned our lesson. Do not piss off an FBI agent, even if she's unarmed."

Logan felt a smile fight through his worry. That was his Ella: tough as nails.

He turned back to her. "Are you really okay?"

She nodded and then, despite all the people watching, she leaned her head on his shoulder and he felt some of the tension seep out of her. "I'm fine. Nothing some aspirin and a bubble bath won't cure."

He got ready to tell her she'd be taking that bubble bath at his place, when he realized that would probably give the officers standing around the wrong impression. Well, at least about his intentions at this particular moment. When she was feeling better, Ella in a bubble bath... Yeah, that did sound like a good idea.

Ella's head lifted and she squinted at him. "What are you thinking?"

Rather than tell her, he got back to the important issue. "What happened?"

"I was in my room when I got a call from Sean Fink."

"Fink?" Logan spat.

"Yeah. He said he was at my hotel, said he had information about the case and wanted to meet. But when I pressed, he claimed he was at the old hotel, not this one. So, I said I'd meet him at the coffee shop by the station. I was on my way over there when the blue van showed up and tried to turn me into roadkill."

Fury flared up. Logan looked around the crowd of officers until he found Hank; because of his size, citizens generally didn't want to mess with him. "Bring Sean Fink in."

"I am definitely on that," Hank said, with enough malice in his tone that Logan knew he was secretly fond of Ella.

"Then what happened?" he asked Ella as Hank and his partner took off.

"I shot at the van, hoping to stop it, and then I jumped." She gestured to the steep embankment on one side of the road. It was dotted with shrubs and small trees and would have been a painful place to land.

"But you're okay?" he asked, needing to hear her confirm it one more time.

She smiled up at him, let him see her clear, focused expression. "I'm really okay, Logan."

"All set," the EMT said, stepping back so Logan could see her arm was taped up.

"Great." Logan helped Ella out of the ambulance. "Then let's move you out of this hotel."

Ella put a hand to her head.

From the slightly unsteady way she was walking, he could tell she was hurting worse than she wanted to admit, making him wish he was the one bringing Sean Fink in. But Ella needed him right now, and that was more important.

"I'm tired." She sighed.

"I know." Logan took her uninjured arm and led her over to one of the cruisers for a ride up to the hotel. "I'm going to get you that aspirin. And then I'm taking you to my place."

So THIS WAS Logan's house.

Ella looked around curiously as Logan led her inside, his arm around her waist as if he was afraid she was going to do something embarrassing like faint. She did feel a little woozy from the bump to her head, but if it had been anyone else, she would have straightened and insisted she was fine. But she liked the feel of Logan's arm around her too much.

So instead, she leaned closer and took in the dark leather furniture filling the living room. There was a large-screen TV in one corner and a bookcase in another. The room was uncluttered, with the exception of photographs on the bookshelf featuring family and friends.

As Logan shut the door behind them, his phone started beeping. He set her bag on the floor and, keeping a firm grip on her waist, pulled the phone out of his pocket.

He looked at it, then tucked it away again. "That was Hank. He texted me to say Fink is in custody."

"Good." Ella twisted her head to look up at him. "You're not going, are you?" She didn't have the energy to deal with guiding an interrogation right now.

"No. Hank knows not to let him leave. We're going to arrest him and hang on to him until at least tomorrow. I'll deal with him then. Right now, I want to make sure you're okay."

Ella smiled at his concern. One of the other cops had brought Logan's car from the station out to the hotel and it had been waiting when she'd finished grabbing her belongings and checking out. And now she was here, in Logan's house, nervous and filled with a strong sense of anticipation.

As they stepped farther inside, Ella noticed the green plaid chair on the far side of the room, completely at odds with the rest of the furniture. Logan led her to it and helped her sit down.

She smiled up at him, trying not to laugh. "This is the ugliest chair I've ever seen."

Crinkles formed at the corners of Logan's eyes as he crouched low beside her. "It was my grandfather's."

"Oh." Her smile fled. "Sorry."

He grinned. "It's okay. It's the ugliest chair

I've ever seen, too, but after my grandparents passed, I couldn't bear to see it go to Goodwill. I look at it and I always think of him sitting in it. So, I had to bring it home." He pushed her bangs gently out of her eyes. "Besides, it's the most comfortable thing you'll ever sit on."

She went lightheaded at his touch, and it had nothing to do with her injuries. Staring into his green eyes, she suddenly didn't care about the cuts and bruises covering her body. She suddenly didn't care that she would have to leave soon and that once she did, she'd probably never see him again. "Can you get me that aspirin?" she asked, and even to her ears, her voice sounded funny.

Worry filled his eyes as he hurried into the other room.

Ella let out a shaky breath as she stared after him, needing the minute alone to untangle her thoughts. When had this happened? *How* had this happened?

She was in love with Logan Greer.

Of all the crazy things she'd done, falling in love with a homicide detective who lived in a different state, who hadn't even been willing to leave Oakville for a fiancée, was at the top of the list.

Tonight's brush with the blue van had been scary, but she'd been in worse situations before. Lying in the street with a bullet to the leg and a gang member coming for her all those years ago, she'd fully accepted the likelihood that she was going to die. She hadn't wanted to go, had been determined to fight until the end, but she hadn't had the same panicked feeling that had rushed over her today. The feeling that she was leaving something unfinished.

She looked up as Logan hurried back into the room, handing her an aspirin and a glass of water.

"Thanks." She took the aspirin, swallowed it dry, and then pushed herself to her feet.

"Will you give me a tour? Maybe we can start with your bedroom."

LOGAN'S MIND WENT completely and utterly blank.

He tried to get some of his blood flow redirected north as he stared at Ella. Had she just said what he thought she had?

She stood close, staring up at him with hope and anxiety in her eyes.

Just last night, she'd been so determined to resist the attraction between them. Had she hit her head harder than he'd realized? Logan took a small step backward, trying to be a gentleman. "I thought you wanted to get some medicine and get cleaned up?" His words came out choked and too high-pitched.

She must have realized how badly he wanted to grab her hand and run down the hall, because she smiled.

He'd seen a lot of her smiles over the past week. Her teasing grin. Her sad-but-trying-to-hide-it smile. Her full-blown, teeth-showing, happy smile. But he'd never seen this sexy, come-hither grin. It made him want to sink to his knees and do whatever she asked.

She held out her hand. "Okay. I hope your shower is big enough for two."

Logan took her hand, twining their fingers together, and stepped closer, wrapping his other hand around her waist.

"Ella," he whispered. He'd planned to ask her if she was sure, but the way she was looking at him, with need and desire and something else, something that looked a lot like deep, deep affection made him shut up and kiss her. He pressed his lips to hers a little harder than he'd intended, with all the built-up emotion he'd been trying to suppress.

She wound her free hand around his neck and leaned into him, kissing him until his head felt as if it was going to explode.

He pulled back just enough to wrap one arm more securely under her arms and hook the other under her knees. Then, he was carrying her as fast as he could down the hall.

She laughed and the sound rung in his ears as she kept kissing him—his chin, his cheek, his neck, whatever she could reach—as he pushed open the door to his bedroom and carried her to his bed. He lay her down gently and then just stared at her, wanting to freeze this perfect moment.

She belonged here. She belonged with him.

He lowered himself carefully down on top of her, trying not to bump any of her bruises. Then, he brushed her hair back, letting his fingers slide through it, wanting to memorize every single detail of the night. He hooked his fingers through hers and found her neck with his mouth.

"I wish we had more time," he whispered as he licked his way up to her earlobe. "I'd like to take you out to my family's cabin, on the ocean, and do nothing but make love to you for a week straight."

Ella made a sound that could have been agreement or desire, as her fingers broke free of his and sank into his hair, pulling his lips back to hers. Then her tongue was in his mouth and he couldn't speak at all, could barely think.

Her hands slid around his back and he could feel them up under his T-shirt. He helped her pull it over his head and then reached for hers, letting his hands glide over her smooth skin on the way up.

When he tossed the T-shirt aside, he discovered she was wearing a black lace bra. For some reason, he'd expected something more basic, like a sports bra. He made a noise of appreciation in the back of his throat, the only sound he was still capable of making, and she laughed at him again.

Until he lowered his head and pressed his mouth between her breasts. Then, her laughter turned into a moan as she arched up toward him. He slid his hands down over her rib cage, careful of the cut slicing her left side, as he circled his hands around her tiny waist. Then he felt her strong hands gripping him, trying to pull his mouth back to hers. He smiled against her skin and kissed his way slowly downward instead as his fingers found the button on her jeans.

She lifted her hips as he slipped her jeans down her long legs and tossed them aside. Then he slid his hand up one leg as his mouth traveled the same path on the other leg until she was squirming beneath him and his lips hit her hip. And, oh jeez, her panties were the same black lace as her bra.

His eyes must have rolled back in his head, because she gave him that sexy smile again and whispered, "I have a pair in every color."

Logan started at her belly button and licked a fast line up to her lips. Then, with his mouth locked on hers, and her hands on his hips, fitting him against her just right, his whole body started throbbing with need.

"Logan," she moaned. She was reaching between them, trying to get his pants off, when they both flinched as his phone started beeping from his pocket.

"Ignore it," he mumbled against her mouth, kicking his pants free and rocking against her until she arched toward him again. Until her fingers dug into his back and she was making encouraging little sounds as her tongue found his.

He slid the straps of her bra down her shoulders and slipped his tongue under the lace. Ella's legs wrapped around his waist, squeezing tight. He was reaching under her back, fumbling for the hook, when his phone buzzed again.

Cursing, Logan forced himself to disentangle his body from Ella's and grabbed his pants, fishing his phone out of his pocket. Two calls so close together probably meant a break in the case.

He had to blink repeatedly to get his eyes to focus on the phone and then he saw it was Becky.

He let out a frustrated groan, looking over at

Ella, her lips swollen and moist from his kisses, her pupils dilated with desire.

"One second," he croaked, pulling up the text in case it was important. They'd worried all along Becky could be a target of the killer's, so he couldn't ignore two frantic texts now, not even with the likely killer in custody.

Logan, can you please come over right away? I'm back at my house and I think someone is here, the first text read.

Logan grabbed his pants with one hand, swearing as he moved on to the second text. Bodyguard sleeping, but I keep hearing noises outside. Probably nothing, but can you please come and check, Lo? *Lo* was the name she'd called him as a kid, back before she could say Logan.

He yanked his pants up his legs and put his T-shirt on inside-out, the way Ella had pulled it off of him. "I'm sorry, Ella. I need to go check on Becky."

She sat up, worry replacing the desire in her eyes. "Is everything okay?"

"Probably." He leaned over and kissed her hard on the mouth, a promise that they'd pick up where they'd left off as soon as he could get back. "I'll hurry. If this really is a problem and I don't get back and you need to go somewhere, my car is in the garage. Keys are by the door, okay?"

"Sure. You want me to come with you?"

Man, did he. "No, it's okay. Get some sleep. I'll put the alarm on when I go."

Shoving his feet back into his shoes, he couldn't keep himself from pressing another kiss to her lips. "I love you," filled his mouth, but he held it back. Now wasn't the time to tell her, when he was leaving. He'd wait until he returned.

And then, screw the challenges of her living in another state. He was going to fight for her.

MAN, HIS SISTER had bad timing.

Logan tried to calm the blood raging through

his veins as he dialed Becky and sped toward her house.

Why was she even there? She had been staying with their parents, she and the bodyguard both, and he didn't like that she'd moved back home without telling him. Still, everything had been fine when he'd checked in with her earlier today. Hopefully, she was just nervous about being back home and hearing things. Hopefully, he could check it out quickly and get back to Ella.

Ella, who was waiting for him in his bed.

That thought sent another shot of lust spiking through his system and he turned the air-conditioning as high as it would go as he reached Becky's neighborhood, not all that far from his own. His call went to voice mail, making him frown and unhook the snap on his holster.

When he pulled into her drive, the house was dark. Even the porch light was off. Something wasn't right.

Logan squinted as he put the car in Park, his

law enforcement instincts kicking into high gear. Her front door was open.

He grabbed the cell phone off his passenger seat to call for backup and opened his car door. He didn't see anyone, but that didn't mean no one was there. Dread felt like a steel ball in his stomach as he raced for the doorway, slipping his phone in his pocket and pulling his gun instead.

Where was his sister?

Even as he was rushing through the door, he knew he should have called for backup first, but this was Becky. And sometimes, every second mattered.

He realized someone was behind him a second before cold metal prongs touched his neck, before electricity shot through his body at way too many volts. Pain instantly darted along his nerve endings. He felt all his limbs stiffen and then shake uncontrollably, his gun slip from his hands, no matter how hard he tried to hang on to it. He felt himself falling before the Taser pressed against his neck a second time. He felt himself hit the floor before it hit him a third.

Then, he blacked out.

Chapter Fifteen

Something was beeping.

Ella groaned and rolled over. She blinked, confused, and then realized where she was. Logan's bedroom. In his bed.

She sat up and looked around. She was alone.

The alarm clock next to Logan's bed read 8:00 a.m. She listened for sounds in the other room, wondering if Logan had come home and she'd slept through it. Disappointment filled her at the idea. But she didn't hear anything. The house was silent.

And then there was the beeping again.

Realizing it was her phone, Ella climbed off the bed, and all the bruises swelling on her body from her roll down the embankment last night protested. She grabbed her jeans off the floor and pulled her phone out, squinting at the readout. She'd missed a text from Logan.

Becky is fine, it read. Fink confessed.

Sean Fink was the killer. Ella sank back on the bed, mad at herself for ruling him out when they'd first talked to him. Even now, after he'd tried to run her off the road last night, she was still slightly surprised, her gut insisting he didn't quite fit the profile.

But at least it was finally over. Oakville was safe.

They wouldn't need her anymore. She could go home, or fly to California and spend a few days on the beach before heading back to work. Neither option sounded appealing.

She wanted Logan. And not just for a night.

Ella blinked back sudden tears and lifted her phone again to read the rest of the text. Fink lawyered up, so we're in a holding pattern. Let's get away. Meet me at my family's cabin.

He'd texted her the address. Ella smiled as she thought of Logan's whispered words from last night: *I'd like to take you out to my family's cabin, on the ocean, and do nothing but make love to you for a week straight.*

Desire and anticipation mingled as Ella grabbed her clothes, ready to get dressed and rush over there. Then, she remembered she hadn't showered since yesterday and she realized she smelled like dirt.

Hurrying into Logan's bathroom, Ella shed her undergarments and got into the shower. It felt intimate to use the soap that smelled like him and made her even more anxious to get to the cabin. To make good on all the promises he'd made last night with his lips and his hands and the look in his eyes.

She'd never gone into any relationship knowing it had an expiration date before. But she'd never fallen in love with anyone like this before, either. This crazy, irresistible pull that kept intensifying with every new detail she learned about him, every strength and even every weakness. Love wasn't supposed to be like this. Lust, maybe, but simple lust didn't come with this much desire to know everything about a person, to spend every minute with them, even if it was talking about a serial killer.

Ella laughed at herself as she realized she'd been smiling since she'd stepped into the shower, preparing to see Logan. Wow, she had it bad.

Drying off fast, Ella wrapped the towel around herself and ran into Logan's living room to grab her bag. She dug through it until she found a pair of panties and a bra in red lace. A rush of lust filled her system as she imagined how Logan would react to seeing them, and she quickly slipped them on, topping them with a skirt and tank top. She left her gun in her bag and took it with her as she turned off Logan's alarm, grabbed his keys and got into his convertible.

As she raced through the streets, following his

navigation system to the address he'd sent her, she felt downright euphoric at the prospect of seeing Logan. Downright euphoric at the idea of wrapping her arms and legs around him until they both passed out from pleasure. And just downright euphoric at her intense love for him, no matter what happened in the future.

She'd take short-term with Logan over the rest of her life with someone else.

Winding down streets that took her out of Oakville, Ella kept pressing her foot harder on the gas. Forget checking out the cabin, forget looking out at the undoubtedly amazing view together. As soon as she saw Logan, she was going to tell him with her body all the things she was too scared to say out loud.

Way to play it cool, Cortez, her mind screamed, while another part of her brain whispered, *Coward.*

Ella bit her lip as she turned down a long, private road. Could she bring herself to tell him how she felt? Would it make any difference?

The navigation system led her to the last house on the road, a little two-story all-wood cabin with a wraparound porch. It was pretty, nestled in the woods and raised up off the ground, but it wasn't at all what she'd expected his family to own. She'd assumed it would be another fancy Southern-style home that was more mansion that true cabin. But this did remind her a little of the lived-in part of his parents' house, cozy and comfortable and meant for spending time together.

Ella stepped out of the convertible and took the steps up to the cabin two at a time. She was smiling so hard her face actually hurt.

The door was unlocked and when Ella pushed it open, there were rose petals leading into the darkened house, lit by candles scattered on the tabletops and sunlight streaming in the windows, filtered through the woods.

The woods. Ella faltered, ice racing up her spine. Logan had said his family's cabin was on the ocean.

She spun around, ready to race back to the car, back to her bag, which held her gun. But a man was standing there, just far enough from the light that he was bathed in shadows. She didn't know who he was, but he wasn't Logan.

Ella shifted her stance and lifted her fists. If her options were fight or run, today she picked fight. She didn't know this house, didn't know where another exit was, or if it would be blocked.

Fear shot through her, and not just for herself. It hadn't been Logan who'd texted her.

She had a sudden realization of how the killer was targeting his victims, how he was getting them to meet him in a deserted location: hacking their phones and pretending to be someone else.

It would explain how he'd crafted the perfect message to her, too. He'd probably seen the real message from Hank, telling Logan that Fink was in custody.

But right now, the only thing that mattered was that it hadn't been Logan texting her.

So where was Logan? Was he hurt? Was he dead?

A sob welled up and Ella pushed it back as the figure got closer, stepping into the light. She didn't recognize him.

She readied herself to fight, calling on all the training the FBI had drilled into her during her eighteen weeks at the Academy.

Then he pulled his hand from behind his back and fast, too fast, something was swinging toward her head.

Ella ducked and spun, trying to dart around the killer, to get out the door.

But he was quick for his size and he blocked her way and swung again. The block of wood flew past her as she darted backward, throwing herself off balance. And then he was swinging again, before she got her equilibrium back.

His next swing caught her on the arm and sent

her flying. She crashed to the floor, sliding into the staircase.

Immediately, she flipped over, tried to push herself to her feet, and then the wood was coming at her again. It struck her temple and pain exploded in her head.

Bile filled Ella's throat and the room dimmed around her. As she felt herself losing the battle for consciousness, the killer stepped over her and raised the wood again.

She tried to lift her hands to block the blow, but they wouldn't move.

And then everything went dark.

Consciousness returned slowly, painfully. When Ella forced her eyes open, the ceiling was blurry, moving with every beat of her heart. Her head throbbed so badly she was nauseated.

She was sitting on a chair, her head lolling over the back. When Ella tried to move her head, tried to shift so she could see where she was, she realized her arms and legs wouldn't move. She was tied to the chair.

Fear skittered along her nerve endings. How long had she been out? Was she still in the cabin? Where was Logan? Where was the killer?

She heard a low, pained moan and wondered who else was in the room until she realized it was her making the noise. Sucking in a deep breath, Ella used all her strength to move her head, so she could look around. Another groan ripped from her throat as her forehead throbbed harder and a stream of blood slid down her cheek.

She was hurt worse than she'd realized. She probably had a concussion. The right side of her forehead felt swollen to the size of a grapefruit and there was a haze over her eyes.

Ella blinked and squinted, trying to get her bearings. She was in a room, probably a bedroom, though the chair she was sitting on was the only furniture. The shades were down on the sole window, but she was pretty sure she was still in the cabin, probably upstairs now.

She listened hard, trying to determine whether the killer had left, but all she could hear was a buzzing in her ears that she suspected was connected to her head injury.

Then a form filled the doorway and Ella swallowed back a scream. He was blurry through her clouded vision, but he was big. Not quite Hank O'Connor big, but close.

"You're awake," he snarled, stepping closer.

Ella blinked and blinked until her vision started to clear, until she could make out his face. Light blue eyes, sandy blond hair, average features. She didn't recognize him. But the look in his eyes told her all she needed to know: he was planning to kill her.

Why hadn't he done it yet? Why had he bothered to knock her out and tie her up? Bile rose up her throat. Did he plan to burn and torture her like he had his victims?

The idea made tears rush forward, but Ella

held them in, staring him dead in the eyes. If he was a sadist, he wanted her afraid, and she refused to give it to him. Not that easily.

As if he could read her mind, as if he was anticipating her taking the hard way, he smiled. A slow, calculating curve of his mouth that made her want to shrink backward.

But there was nowhere to go.

Ella tugged at the bonds tying her hands behind her back, but they were tight, digging into her wrists. Her ankles were latched to the legs of the chair equally tightly.

He watched her test them, then laughed, a deep, guttural sound. "Believe me, I know how to tie a knot. Don't bother."

Ella forced words through her dry mouth. "Who are you?"

He scowled at her and the average, unmemorable features became a dark mask of fury. "You should know. You came looking for me."

Ella ran through the options in her head, the

people she had specifically questioned. "You work for Adam Pawlter, don't you?"

"And it's a waste of my time," he spat, his scowl deepening.

Ella squinted at him, trying to read him. "But it works for you. It's physical work, but it doesn't take too much mental energy. It gives you time with your fantasies. You've had them a long time, haven't you? Probably most of your life."

"Trying to profile me?" he asked darkly, pulling off his long-sleeved T-shirt and tossing it aside as if he was about to get physical.

"Burns," Ella murmured. His face was untouched, but the burn marks covered his arms completely down to his elbow, disappearing up under the sleeves of his undershirt. She'd been right. And the fact that he had burn scars meant he burned his victims for a personal reason, maybe not to torture them, but for some other gratification. Maybe to make them look like him.

He stepped close, bracing his hands on her

arms, making her twitch with the desire to break away from his touch. Then he leaned down so his eyes were inches from hers. He smelled like ocean brine and smoke.

Ella tried not to flinch.

"Yes, I have burns. You planning to analyze me, profiler? Maybe we should talk about why I burn them." His voice dropped low, almost to a growl. "You want me to show you? You want to see how it feels?"

"No," Ella croaked, panic erupting. Was this where Theresa and Laurie had died? Tied to this chair, begging for their lives?

She needed to get him on a new subject, fast. But what would distract him?

"How did you lure them to you? That's what I couldn't figure out," she said quickly, even though she already knew. She was betting that he'd want to brag about how clever he was. She could tell by the sick smile spreading across his face when she asked that he loved feeling the power he gained from tricking his victims.

Then his eyes narrowed, as though he knew what she was doing. He pushed himself away from the chair and said, "They thought they were meeting someone else. Just like you did."

"You hacked their phones."

"Yes." Amusement flickered in his eyes. "I got the idea a few years ago. It took me a while to figure it out. I had to make a rather unsavory friend, get him to teach me. Then he hooked me up with his spoofing service, made that part real simple for me. And the connection turned out to be mutually beneficial."

"Why?" Ella asked, not sure she wanted to know the answer. Had he killed for someone else, too? It wouldn't fit his self-centered needs, but maybe it had given him a chance to practice.

"It's not what you're thinking. I just gave him an alibi. He doesn't know what I do. And now I've got something to hold over his head. Just in case."

"What about Theresa and Laurie? Tell me about them."

"They were so stupid. They got the texts and neither of them bothered to call and verify. I didn't think they would. I was very, very careful with the wording, to make it sound like the person they expected." He smiled, baring his teeth, and the light that came into his eyes was unnatural and evil. "They came right to me. And then it was too late for them."

"It was you who texted Logan," she realized.

"Of course. Becky is still at her parents' house, safe and sound. At least for now. But I knew he'd go running to save her. He made it so easy. I actually thought he might have been more of a challenge, being a *detective* and all. And you." He shook his head. "You were pitiful. Running up the stairs like that, the look on your face when you saw the rose petals I put out for you."

Shivers inched up Ella's skin. Where was Logan now? The need to ask was overwhelming, but she was terrified of the answer. And terrified that if by some miracle he was still alive, she shouldn't remind the killer.

How had he known Logan had told her about the cabin? Hacking Logan's phone might have told him Sean Fink was in custody, but it wouldn't have told him about the cabin. Had he been listening at Logan's house last night? The thought made her time with Logan feel tainted.

She desperately wanted to ask if Logan was okay, but she forced herself not to, forced herself to ask instead, "How did you know to mention a cabin?"

He smiled, that creepy, self-satisfied smile that made Ella want to knock it off his face. "I followed Theresa all week. I knew as soon as I saw her that I wanted her. I thought she was going to be perfect." His smile fell off. "But she wasn't. She wasn't perfect at all."

"You overheard her talk about the cabin?"

"I overheard Becky telling her all kinds of things. About her grandparents' house in Huntsville, about the family cabin on the ocean, about her nickname for her brother." He leaned close to her again, so close that she could feel his breath on her face. "Becky could be perfect, too. I don't know yet."

A new sort of fear rushed through her. She couldn't let anything happen to Logan's little sister. Even if he was gone, he would want her to try to protect Becky.

The thought that Logan could already be dead, that she'd never see his green eyes sparkling with laughter or desire again, that she'd never have the chance to tell him she loved him, made her feel as if she was choking. As if all the air had been sucked out of the room and her heart was compensating by beating faster and faster.

She was having a panic attack, she realized as her head dropped to her chest. She'd never had one in her life, but that had to be what this was.

Get it together, Cortez.

She focused on slowing her heart rate, on evening out her breathing, and tried not to think about anything beyond getting out of this chair. She'd worry about everything else afterward.

But how could she get free?

She knew her best chance was to keep him talking, learn as much as she could about how he thought, and then try to use it against him, use it to get him to make a mistake. From the BAU office, she did that all the time. Analyzed killers and told the police how to make them slip up. But the stakes had never been her own life, the lives of people she loved.

Ella jerked her head back up and the room spun. When it straightened out, the killer was staring at her, studying her.

"You don't want anything to happen to Becky," he said in flat tone. "Or to Logan."

Ella felt tears rush to her eyes with relief. Logan was still alive.

"But you should have thought of that before you talked to Adam. Before you stopped by the dock and called me. You're way too persistent. The other guys never ask why I keep my shirt on out on the ocean. They just figure I'm out of shape and embarrassed. But if the cops started asking about burns, it might have come out that I stay covered up. It might have made you suspect me specifically. I can't have you digging around anymore." He walked around behind her and she felt his hand slide underneath her head to grab the back of the chair.

Then the chair tilted backward and he was dragging her through the doorway as the whole world spun. He pulled the chair down the hall and then kicked open the door to another room, yanking her inside and setting the chair straight again.

When she had her equilibrium back, she saw she wasn't alone.

Tied to the chair next to her was Logan. She didn't see any immediate injuries, but his head lolled to the side, his eyes closed. It was only by staring intently that she could see his chest faintly rising and falling, and confirm that he really was alive.

"Logan," she breathed.

But he remained silent and still.

"He had no idea until you showed up in town," the killer spat at her. "I would have left him alone. It's your fault. Remember that."

"No." Ella shook her head frantically and pain burst behind her eyes. "We have someone else in custody. You know that." She sounded desperate, even to her own ears.

"It was only a matter of time before you realized Sean Fink wasn't smart enough to do this." A half smile formed on his lips. "You're quick." The smile dropped off and was replaced by a dark scowl. "You shot the van. That's going to be a problem. But if you'd just been easier to kill, we wouldn't be in this situation right now."

"No," Ella protested. "It's not—"

He shrugged. "It's too late now, profiler. You're going to have to disappear. Both of you."

Chapter Sixteen

He heard Ella's voice. It was coming from a great, great distance, and Logan struggled to reach it, fighting the blackness that threatened to pull him under again.

As his mind cleared, he started to remember. Going to Becky's house and being ambushed. He'd woken again, trussed up in the back of a van that smelled like shrimp, bouncing along the road, not knowing where he was headed. As soon as the van had opened and the killer had realized he was awake, Logan had gotten stunned with the Taser again, then hit in the head with something.

It had happened a fifth time when he'd come

to in the bedroom of a cabin. And then he'd stayed under. For how long, he had no idea.

But if he could hear Ella... He prayed it was just his unconscious mind wishing for her, that she wasn't really here, but even before he pried his eyes open, he knew she was. He could sense her beside him.

And as his eyes focused, there she was. Tied to the chair next to him, the right side of her forehead swollen, blood streaking over her cheek. "Ella," he rasped.

"Logan." She sounded so relieved, and more clear-headed than he was, despite her injury.

Logan forced his head to lift, and his spine creaked in protest after too long with his head hanging sideways. He drew in a deep breath, trying to get his mind to focus. The air felt thick and noxious, and he tried to identify why, but all he could focus on was Ella. "Are you okay?"

It wasn't Ella who answered. "Neither of you are going to be okay for much longer."

Logan turned his head to face forward. Fury

rushed through him that the killer had hurt Ella, and it helped clear the cobwebs in his brain. "Marshall."

Adam's nephew nodded. "So, you know me. I wasn't sure if you would."

"Why? Why would you do this?"

Marshall tilted his head, his lips stretching into something that might be called a smile if it wasn't so filled with malice. "Why would I abduct and murder young women? Or why would I kidnap you and your profiler girlfriend?"

Marshall sounded so calm, as though this was a normal conversation.

How had no one around him noticed he was totally nuts?

Logan cursed himself for not following up more aggressively on Marshall and the rest of Adam's shrimping crew. If he had, maybe he and Ella wouldn't be here right now. Maybe they'd still be back at his place, tangled together in his sheets, making plans for the future.

Now would they even have a future?

Logan tugged at the knots around his wrists, trying to be subtle about it. "Why would you do any of it?"

And what was Marshall planning to do with them now? Why were they here, tied up in some cabin in the woods instead of already gator food?

Marshall sighed, looking bored with the question, with him. "The profiler over there already wanted to know about the burns." A light came into his eyes. "You want to talk about the burns?"

Logan studied the dark brown, raised scars on Marshall's arms, remembering what Ella had said about the killer having burns himself. Judging from the too-excited expression on Marshall's face, burns were a topic to stay far away from. "Not really."

Man, the knots around his wrists were tight. Trying to stretch them was just slicing into his skin. But of course, Marshall was a sailor. He would know how to tie a proper knot.

Logan glanced around for anything to work with in case Marshall left them alone, but the room was mostly empty. It just held the chairs he and Ella were sitting on and old newspapers, crumpled up on the floor around them. And his ankles seemed to be tied as tightly as his wrists.

"Don't bother," Marshall said. "You think I'd leave anything nearby that you could use to get yourself out of those knots?" He shook his head. "I'm not stupid. Even though I took your gun from you at your sister's house, I'm not taking chances."

Becky. A new worry filled him. "Where is she?"

"Your sister?" Marshall smiled again, this one an anticipatory smile that made Logan's skin crawl. "She's still at your parents' house, I assume. She never really went back home."

Insight flashed through him. "It was you on the phone." It had been Marshall all along. That was why Theresa had gone to meet him. She'd thought she was meeting Becky. The second number on Theresa's cell phone records that had looked as if it came from Becky had actually been Marshall. Logan swore, a string of offensive names that just made Marshall shake his head.

"That's not nice," Marshall said, taking a step toward him, pulling the Taser from his pocket.

"I want to know about the burns," Ella suddenly spoke up.

Logan's head whipped toward her. What was she doing?

Her eyes darted fast to his and then back to Marshall, her face never turning, and he realized. She wasn't just trying to prevent Marshall from hitting him with the Taser again. She was profiling Marshall, trying to talk their way out of this. Or at least trying to distract Marshall long enough for Logan to make a move.

As Marshall's attention turned entirely, disturbingly, to Ella, Logan wrenched at his bonds again, but he'd been right before. They were tight, too tight, and all he succeeded in doing was slicing through the skin at his wrists and wetting the rope with his blood.

But as he twisted his hands, he realized they weren't tied to the chair; they were only tied together behind his back. If he lifted his shoulders and shifted forward, he could yank them over the top of the chair. He'd still have his hands tied behind his back, but if he could just get his ankles free…

He'd been a linebacker when he'd played high school and college football. If he could get his ankles free, he wouldn't need his hands. He could rush Marshall. Just use brute strength, go low and twist a shoulder up under his rib cage and then run him straight into the wall as fast and as hard as he could.

He just needed to wait for an opening.

Because Ella was as smart and resourceful as she was gorgeous. If he gave her the chance, if he could hold Marshall down long enough, she could get out. Even tied to her own chair, even with a set of stairs to somehow get down, he knew she could do it.

And as long as she was safe, it didn't really matter what happened to him.

But watching her now as he shifted his legs, trying to see how sturdy the chair was, he realized she'd never leave him there. That just wasn't her style. And although it was one of the things he loved about her, right now he wished she were just a little bit less courageous.

She was staring at Marshall with her chin tipped up and such a challenging expression in her eyes, as if she was daring him to take her on, that it scared him. Because right now, Marshall held all the cards. Not to mention the Taser and Logan's gun.

Marshall ran a finger across Ella's arm with such blatant ownership it made Logan want to shove his chair sideways and slam it into the man as hard as he could. Especially when Ella shivered in disgust. It took all his self-control to remain still, to let Ella use her profiling talent.

"You want to know why I burn them?" His voice dropped to a near whisper. "Or you want to know how?"

"Neither," Ella said, her voice surprisingly strong and even. "I want to know about *your* burns."

Darkness fell over Marshall's face, and Logan watched him carefully, holding his breath as he turned his feet sideways, trying to hook his heels on the sides of the chair legs. But the knots were tight and his heels kept slipping off. Finally, they caught hold, and he pushed outward, testing the strength of the chair legs. They shifted slightly at the pressure.

Marshall took a small step backward. His mouth moved, as though he was having some kind of silent debate, then he said, "Why not? It's not like you'll be telling anyone."

His forehead furrowed, and he looked down at the floor. "There was a fire, back when I was twelve. We were away on vacation. My parents didn't make it. And I got caught in it, too.

But all anyone here knows is that my parents died when I was young. Adam made sure no one knew the details, that no one knew about the fire at all. I told him it was too hard to talk about."

Ella's eyes narrowed. "You set the fire, didn't you?"

His lips stretched a tiny bit as he looked back at Ella. "Not even Adam suspected that."

"But he's always wondered about you, hasn't he? He always knew something wasn't right."

Marshall threw his hands up, made an ugly noise in the back of his throat. "Sure, Adam knows I'm…different, but he doesn't think I killed his sister."

"You did it on purpose, didn't you? Were your parents your first murders?"

Logan glanced over at Marshall, whose mouth darted in and out of a smile as if the memory was a mix of good and bad. Which it probably was.

"They deserved it." His voice rose. "You know

what they did to me?" He took a ragged breath, quieted down to tell her. "My father saw things in me. Things he didn't like. He figured if he beat me enough, I'd stop. I didn't stop. And after they were gone, it was easier. Adam had no idea what I thought about. He never looked on my computer, never wondered what I liked to look at. He doesn't know what I'm doing now."

"But he started to suspect after we talked to him, didn't he?"

Marshall's smile slipped and his tone hardened. "Yes. He hasn't said anything, but I can tell. He knows I've taken the van out at night. He wonders if it might be me."

Ella nodded. "And you found out recently that he's dying."

"You profiling me again? Yeah, now he's dying. And he expects me to take over his stupid business."

"And you don't have time for that," Ella said as Logan worked his feet up and down, frantically trying to fray the rope against the legs of the chair.

He could hear the rope sawing, and it sounded much too loud, but Marshall hadn't looked at him at all since Ella had asked about his burns.

"I only took the job in the first place because it gave me plenty of time to do other things, plenty of time to plan. To imagine what would happen when I took them. But it never goes quite how I picture it." He shrugged, visibly trying to calm down. "But it doesn't matter that Adam wants me to take over the business. It's not happening."

Ella must have figured the conversation was heading in a bad direction, because she asked quickly, "Theresa wasn't the first girl, was she, Marshall?"

Marshall folded his arms over his chest and Logan realized the man had more muscle than he'd originally suspected. Sure, Marshall was big, but big didn't always mean strength. But he should have realized Marshall would be strong, given what he did for a living.

Logan pulled his feet harder inward, making the ropes dig painfully into his ankles, sliding them against the chair faster. He needed his feet free.

"No, Theresa wasn't the first," Marshall said slowly. "Two years ago, I picked up this hitch-hiker. She started telling me about her past, and it was like mine. A lonely childhood, parents who didn't understand her. I thought…" He scowled. "But when I showed her the burns, she looked at me like I was disgusting. And when I burned her, she still didn't get it. So, I got rid of her. Dumped her in the marsh. I worried about it for a long time, thinking the police were going to show up, but they never did."

He laughed and looked over at Logan, who went instantly still.

"You never even knew she was missing, because she wasn't supposed to be here in the first place. And that's how I figured out what

I should do. How I could get away with it. Just wait until they were getting ready to leave before I grabbed them. I thought the second one might work out, but when she didn't..." He shrugged, turned his attention back to Ella. "No one even knew she was missing. Not here anyway. And I waited, took my time, to be sure. I waited months and months. And then I saw Theresa."

Praying Marshall wasn't going to share details about Theresa's death, Logan started slicing his bonds against the chair leg again. It was working. The bonds were fraying. Just not fast enough.

Suspicion filled Marshall's face and he started to look Logan's way again when Ella asked, loudly, "What did you mean, about her working out?"

Marshall looked down at the floor and Logan froze, thinking he might have seen the frayed rope, but then he turned his attention back to Ella and there was something new in his eyes.

Something dark and dangerous that made fear rise up, stronger than ever.

Even Marshall's voice was different when he replied, "When they first come to me, they're happy and smiling and I think they might understand. But then when they see me, really see *me*, they change. They don't want me anymore."

Logan felt disgust curl his lips at Marshall's fantasy that the women he abducted had in any way gone to him voluntarily. Even when they'd first shown up, they'd thought they were meeting someone else and he knew it. Of course he knew it. That was his plan.

Marshall reached into his pocket and pulled something out. He stared at his closed hand as if it had all the answers. "And so I try to show them what it feels like to look this way. I figure if we're the same, they might understand, they might feel for me how I feel about them. So, I give them burns like mine."

His eyes lifted to Ella's, suddenly dead and empty. "But they still don't understand. They're supposed to want me the way I want them. But they don't." He lifted his shoulders. "And so they have to die."

When Marshall opened his palm, Logan saw the lighter there.

Then Marshall flicked the switch on the lighter, firing up a flame. He took a step closer to Ella, and panic took flight in Logan's chest.

No, no, no. His feet weren't free yet. Tears stung the backs of his eyes.

Next to him, Ella's jaw clamped and he could tell she planned to endure it, keep talking, keep giving him time to get free.

But he couldn't do it. He couldn't watch Ella get burned. "Don't touch her!"

Marshall froze, then slowly, very slowly, turned toward Logan. And then, just as slowly, he looked down at Logan's feet, then back up at his face, and smiled. It was a sick, disturbed smile. He'd known all along what Logan was doing.

Anger tensed Logan's arms. Forget distraction. There was no way this pathetic excuse for a man was burning Ella. Not while Logan had breath left in his body.

He put every ounce of disgust and contempt he was feeling into his voice. "What kind of coward burns women?"

Next to him, Ella made a noise of distress at his tactic, but he kept his attention focused on Marshall, silently willed Ella to start working on her own ropes.

Rage flickered in Marshall's eyes, but he was still eerily calm as he took a step toward Logan. "You think you can distract me better than she could?" He snorted. "You think you're better than me? Smarter than me?" His voice picked up volume, then quieted down again as he said, "No."

He took another step toward Logan, flicking the lighter on and off.

Keep coming, Logan willed Marshall, as he heard Ella frantically using her chair to saw at the ropes on her ankles.

Marshall glanced briefly at Ella. "There's no time for that," he said, monotone, but Ella kept working on her ropes.

He looked at Logan and flicked the lighter back on. "I never wanted her, you know. Your profiler. If she hadn't come looking for me, I wouldn't have come for either of you. But you don't have to worry. I'm not going to burn her."

He took a step back, away from Logan. "Not like that. No, you both need to disappear. And the marsh isn't going to work. Not for what I have in mind for you two. That would be too easy, too quick a death." He scowled, directing a dark glare at Ella. "You ruined everything and I'm going to punish you for that."

Then he looked pointedly up at the ceiling and Logan's gaze followed to the wood beams up there. "No, this isn't like Theresa at all. This is like my parents."

Dread settled low in Logan's stomach as he finally identified the scent he'd noticed when he'd first regained consciousness. Gasoline—

it was probably on the newspapers. It wasn't strong, so there couldn't have been a lot, but that wouldn't matter. He glanced quickly down at Ella's feet. She had too far to go on the ropes.

And Marshall planned to set the cabin on fire. The wooden cabin that would burn fast, with them trapped inside.

Chapter Seventeen

"You really think you can get away with that?" Logan demanded, yanking his feet inward hard, not caring anymore that Marshall knew what he was doing. "You kill us in your cabin and there'll be no question it was you."

Marshall laughed, a deep, booming sound that suggested he'd come totally unhinged. He kept flicking the lighter—on, off, on, off. "This isn't my cabin."

"Whose is it?" Ella demanded, frantically working on her own ropes.

But neither of them was going to get free. Not in time. And they all knew it.

Panic and regret mingled as Logan wished

he'd taken more care going into Becky's house. That he'd just ignored his beeping phone in the first place, and kept focusing on learning the curves of Ella's body. That he'd told Ella how he felt, before they ran out of time.

"It's Fink's cabin," Marshall said, flipping the lighter up in the air and catching it. "I don't think he'll mind us using it, since he's in custody and all."

"That kind of ruins the frame-up, doesn't it?" Logan asked desperately, still tugging hard at the ropes on his feet. But they weren't breaking. "Sean's not going to be a suspect."

"No." Marshall shrugged. "But maybe the cops will think he's got a partner. I know you're the only ones who suspected me. Besides Adam, but he's dying anyway. And if it looks like the other cops are getting too close, I'll disappear, too. I'll figure it out if I have to."

He glanced down at Logan's feet and then his eyebrows jerked up. "You're better than I expected. I almost got distracted with all this talking." He sighed. "But it's time to go."

"No!" Ella screamed, lurching to her feet. She was still tethered to the chair and she was hunched over awkwardly, barely maintaining her balance as she inched closer to Marshall.

Surprise flashed across Marshall's face and he took a quick step back. Then he seemed to realize what he was doing and he strode forward, got in Ella's face, and flicked the flame on the lighter way too close to her cheek, madness in his eyes. "You want me to start the burns early? Once I set this place on fire, the smoke might get you before the flames. But I can make sure you feel the fire."

Logan looked down at his ankles. The right one was closer to being free, so he shifted his weight left, then pulled his right foot in and kicked it out again as hard as he could.

Agony ripped up from his ankle and something definitely tore, but the chair leg came loose from the seat. Then his weight shifted and the chair crashed down on the right side. The back of the chair slammed into his upper arms as he hit the floor at an awkward angle.

Panic flashed in Marshall's eyes as Logan thrust himself to his feet, still attached to the broken chair by both ankles.

Marshall jerked away, but not before Ella head-butted him, sending him stumbling backward across the room. But he got his balance back fast, not going down, lighter still in hand. He flicked it on as Logan hobbled toward him as fast as he could.

He picked up speed, ignoring the pain shooting up his leg from his ankle. Instead of tackling Marshall low like he'd planned, he hit him full-on, just slammed into him and kept going.

The lighter flew out of Marshall's hand and Logan heard a whoosh behind him as the flame caught something.

Logan kept shoving. With his hands behind his back and his ankles still attached to the chair, he didn't have the momentum to do any real damage if he slammed Marshall into the wall, so Logan twisted his shoulders and angled the other way.

Marshall got his hands up and tried to push Logan off. But Marshall's massive upper body strength wasn't enough to overcome the desperation and fury fueling Logan, with the image of Marshall holding a lighter up to Ella's face imprinted on his brain.

With an inch of space suddenly between them, Marshall smiled, probably thinking he had the upper hand again. But it gave Logan the perfect amount of room to put one last burst of power into his final hit.

He slammed into Marshall as hard as he could and Marshall flew backward, right into the window. Glass shattered, showering Logan as Marshall fell, his scream tearing through the air.

For a second, Logan thought he was going to fall out headfirst, too, but he regained his balance as the oxygen rushed in.

And then there was another, bigger whooshing sound behind him and heat rushed up his back. When he spun around, he saw that the entire room was on fire.

The newspapers that had been scattered across the floor had gone up fast, then jumped to the curtains, and now flames were licking the ceiling. Ella was still near the center of the room, surrounded by flames, slamming her chair up and down against the floor, trying to break it. But it wasn't happening.

Logan lurched toward her, desperately trying to yank his hands free, but they were tied too tightly behind his back. He sucked in a breath full of smoke that made his lungs burn and his eyes water.

"Go!" she screamed at him, then started coughing violently. Tears were streaking down her face and he knew she was struggling to get enough oxygen. "The whole place is going to go up," she gasped as he finally reached her side.

Smoke swirled in the air around them, and Logan could feel the fire singeing his skin even though it wasn't touching him yet. He was moving too slowly with the chair broken and dragging behind him, attached to his legs. He wasn't sure he'd make it out at his speed and Ella was going to be much, much slower.

"Logan," she hacked as he looked around for another option.

But the door was the only way out. When Marshall had gone through the window, he'd hit the branches of a tree before landing a story below directly on the concrete patio. It was possible he'd survived the fall, but it seemed unlikely.

"Get out of here," Ella insisted, moving painfully slowly toward the door. She pressed her chin down near her chest to suck in a breath, then said, "Now! Go!"

"I'm sorry, Ella," Logan choked out. Then he hobbled past her, reaching back to grab her chair with his bound hands, and pulled her with him.

His shoulders ached as he yanked her out the

door as fast as his feet could go, but slowly, too slowly. Their chairs slapped together, tripping him up, and he nearly fell over and over as he lurched down the hallway toward the stairs. He could feel his throat closing up as it clogged with smoke. The stairwell looked far away through vision that was blurring and shifting.

His lungs felt as though they were on fire, and his face felt swollen around his eyes. His mind was starting to go fuzzy from lack of oxygen. If it had just been him, he might have given up, given in to the intense desire to stop, close his eyes and rest.

But Ella was behind him. He could feel her head loll against his hands and he thought she'd lost consciousness, but he couldn't stop to check.

Finally, he reached the stairs. Carefully, he lowered one foot onto the top stair, stretching the ropes, trying to get balanced. But it was no use.

He toppled forward, and pitched face-first down the stairs.

He turned his head in time to avoid doing a face-plant on the edge of the stair, but the side of his head slammed into a step, and then he was lying at the bottom of the stairs, his legs twisted awkwardly behind him, Ella's chair on top of him squeezing out what little oxygen he had left.

Logan's vision blurred and blackened.

Move, his mind demanded. But he felt paralyzed, not enough oxygen getting into his lungs to power his muscles. When he tried to push off the stairs with his feet, nothing happened.

He sucked in a deep breath, but got mostly smoke. He couldn't even seem to cough anymore. His body wasn't working right. His lungs screamed, shooting such intense pain through him that he thought he was going to pass out.

But his vision came back just enough to see the door. It was so close. Only a few feet away.

But it seemed way too far. He could barely think, let alone move.

Then a weight shifted on his hands, a lock of hair falling across his arm. *Ella.*

Logan willed all his energy to his feet and pushed. This time, he and Ella scooted forward, tumbling the rest of the way off the stairs. Her chair shifted sideways, off him, and Logan fumbled for a hold on it again.

He managed to get to his knees, his shoulders and head pressed against the floor, and then he pulled and pulled, but nothing happened. He tried again, and this time, they inched toward the door.

He'd have to stand to open it. On his knees, Logan stared up at the doorknob, his throat and lungs burning, his eyes swollen nearly shut and his vision dotted with black. Despair filled him. Had he come this close not to be able to open the door?

Letting go of Ella's chair, he inched forward on his knees, but he couldn't get to his feet. So, he pressed his shoulder over the doorknob, which was a lever-style. It moved down, then bounced back up, not catching.

He didn't have much time left. He could feel his whole body starting to shut down as every breath he took contained less and less oxygen, more and more smoke.

He shoved down with his shoulder again, hard. He knew he didn't have the strength to get to his feet, so he turned, bent low and raised his hands as high as he could behind his back, pulling the door open.

Fresh air should have come in, but upstairs, the fire was spreading, and smoke swirled down toward them, darker and darker. Logan still couldn't get any air into his lungs.

He leaned back to grab Ella and he fell, the back of his head hitting the floor and his knees aching. Beneath him, more of the chair broke, making it easier to get purchase on the floor. He twisted to put his feet down flat and dragged himself along, pulling Ella with him.

Somehow, he got them out the door, and they

rolled down the steps together, landing in a tangled heap at the bottom.

Ella's eyes were closed and he couldn't see well enough to tell if she was breathing.

He knew he needed to move them farther away, knew the whole cabin was going to go up soon, but as he tried to suck in fresh air, it felt as though he was choking. As though his lungs were so filled with smoke, there was no room for oxygen.

He kept gasping for breath anyway. And then he lost his battle for consciousness and slipped into the darkness.

Epilogue

"He's awake."

Relief rushed through Ella so strongly that tears streaked down her cheeks as she nodded her thanks to the nurse who'd come out to the waiting room to tell her.

It had been three days since she and Logan had been caught in the fire. She didn't remember much after Logan had grabbed her chair, tipped her backward and started hauling her through the house. She recalled watching the flames get closer, thinking they'd never make it. She recalled feeling an overwhelming sadness that she wouldn't get the chance to tell Logan she loved him. And she recalled gasping in a deep breath to tell him while she still could, then choking on the smoke, and fighting the blackness that had come over her.

Apparently, the blackness had won. The next thing she knew, she'd been lying on the ground outside the burning house, an EMT leaning over her.

They'd told her she'd stopped breathing, that they'd revived her on scene as they fought to contain the fire. They'd finally put out the flames, but not before the second story collapsed.

They'd found Marshall's body out back, dead from his fall out the second-story window. Since then, Adam had been making a lot of noise about a frame-up, claiming his nephew couldn't possibly be the killer, but Ella had let Chief Patterson deal with that. She'd gone straight to the hospital and stayed there.

Ella pushed herself to her feet, and standing after so many hours in the plastic hospital chair made her sway. She'd been praying for three days straight that Logan would make it.

Around the room, cops from the Oakville PD who had been taking turns waiting at the hospital stood, too, and started walking toward the nurse.

Beside her, Maggie clutched her elbow. On her other side, Scott wrapped a steadying arm around her shoulder. They'd both flown out as soon as she'd called them, frantic and nearly hysterical with fear.

"He's okay," Maggie reminded her, blue eyes clear and strong despite what she was dealing with, the continuing contact from her rapist and the upcoming anniversary Ella had hoped to cancel by coming here. Two weeks ago, she'd been so certain she'd get a shot at bringing down the Fishhook Rapist. But he was still out there, and September first was coming fast.

As Ella looked at Maggie, even after telling her the truth about why she'd originally come to Florida, she knew her friend wasn't thinking about that right now.

Maggie grinned at her. "Let's go meet your detective."

"Come on," Scott said, a smile in his voice as he helped propel her behind the nurse, toward the patient area. "I've got to meet the man who finally made you fall in love."

But the nurse held up a hand as the three of them reached the doorway and the cops crowded behind her. "Sorry. Just family."

Ella shook her head, ready to wage a huge protest when the nurse added, "Come on, Ella."

Maggie pressed a kiss to the side of her head and Scott patted her back. She even felt Hank's massive paw rest briefly on her shoulder as she moved forward. She looked back at them as she followed the nurse out of the waiting room, and they were all smiling, all so happy for her.

But Logan had been in bad shape. The fact that she'd stopped breathing, which meant she hadn't inhaled as much smoke, had actually worked to her advantage. Once they'd revived her, she'd had her head patched up and stayed overnight for observation.

But Logan had required intubation and he'd been in ICU, so she couldn't even sit in the room with him. They'd told her they didn't know if he was going to wake up again.

She couldn't help sobbing as she remembered, and the nurse gave her an understanding smile. "He's looking good. He's breathing on his own, and next to that, the broken ankle and torn shoulder and the minor burns are nothing. He'll be fine."

Ella drew in a calming breath and wiped away her tears. "Does his family know?"

They'd spent most of the past three days waiting with her, but they'd decided to take a break about half an hour ago, and left to get dinner. They'd wanted her to come along, but she hadn't been able to bear leaving. She'd been afraid that if she did, it would be like breaking some kind of fragile connection and Logan would be gone. It was ridiculous, but her friends had understood and stayed with her.

"We just called them. They're on their way back now."

"Thank you." His family had been so optimistic, so certain Logan would pull through. They'd spent the days talking about all the things they wanted to tell him when he woke up, making plans for Ella to come back and visit him as though it was a given that she would. And the whole time Ella had been paralyzed with fear.

A new sort of fear inched forward now, a fear of losing him from her life. But at least he was alive. And she wasn't giving up without a fight. She was putting everything on the line and seeing where it got her.

She'd never been so terrified.

"Go ahead," the nurse said, holding open the door to Logan's room.

"Ella," Logan rasped as soon as she stepped through the door. He looked pale and exhausted in the hospital bed, an IV running into his arm and hooked up to all kinds of monitors.

But he was finally awake. A smile broke across her face and the tears fell again, racing down her cheeks until she was gasping.

"Hey," he said, holding out his hand. "Come here."

She stepped forward, put her hand carefully in his, and he laced their fingers together, holding tightly enough that she knew he was really going to be okay. She brushed her tears away, embarrassed. "I was so worried."

He smiled at her, and she had to lean down and place a kiss on his forehead, then another and another.

"Come here." He shifted on the bed, obviously trying to suppress a noise of discomfort as he made room for her.

"Be careful," she said as he insisted, "Get in."

"I don't know if—"

"Ella." He locked those green eyes on hers, steady and clear and full of...

Her breath caught. Could it be love she saw there?

He tugged on her hand. "Get in."

She climbed cautiously into the bed beside him, trying not to jostle him, and he laughed, a raw, raspy laugh, and pulled her close.

Wow, she loved this man. It was crazy and unexpected and so, so right. And it was time to tell him.

"Logan..." She cut herself off, realizing she couldn't do this with her head against his chest. She needed to look him in the eyes.

So she propped herself up on her elbow and, her heart beating a frantic staccato, said, "Logan, I don't know how or when this happened, but I..." Nerves flared up and she smiled at him, stared directly into those eyes that had pulled her like a magnet from the day she'd met him. "I love you."

He smiled back at her, a great big grin that told her she hadn't made a fool of herself.

"Ella." He slid his hand from her shoulder

up to her head, pulled her down to press a soft kiss to her lips. Then he continued to hold her close, her face millimeters from his as he told her, "I love you, too."

Joy seemed to burst inside her. She gave a laugh full of happiness, then got serious. "Logan, I want to make this work. I know long-distance isn't easy, but—"

He was already shaking his head. "I don't want to do this halfway, Ella. I want to give us a real chance. With our jobs, long-distance… We'd both get pulled into cases and have to cancel flights and miss visits all the time. I don't want to see you on random weekends. I want you next to me every day."

Ella let out a heavy breath. "Logan, maybe down the line, but…" Her shoulders sank, weighted down by the realities of trying to make this work. "I can't just up and move. I'd have to put in a request to go to a different office and the FBI would have to approve it. That can take months, waiting for a spot to open. I can't be a profiler anywhere else, either. BAU is in Virginia. And I can't leave Maggie. Not right now."

She stared into his eyes, willing him to understand.

He lifted her hand to his lips and pressed a kiss to it. "Ella, I meant that I was thinking of moving to Virginia. Your job may not move, but I *can* be a homicide detective anywhere. Yeah, I might have to take a downgrade initially, but I'll work my way back up fast. I got a detective slot once, even with a chief who can't stand me. I'll get it again." He grinned. "Heck, I'll even let you tell Hank he gets my spot here. If you ever need a favor in this state again, he'll make sure it happens."

Her eyes widened. He was willing to leave Oakville? For her? "Really?" she whispered.

He smiled at her, a soft smile full of love. "Really."

Tears welled up in her eyes again, tears of

joy, and she blinked them back. "Your family is going to hate me," she joked.

"I kind of think they saw this coming. Trust me, they'll be happy for us." His tone turned teasing. "And besides, Mom will just call you every week and ask about grandkids."

Kids with Logan. The thought made anticipation and happiness fill her until she knew she was grinning like an idiot. "Okay. Let's do it." She felt a laugh bubble up. "I've even got room in my den for your ugly old chair."

He tilted his head, his expression serious. "You want to live together?"

Oh, no. She'd misunderstood him. Moving to Virginia was a big enough step, especially considering the short time they'd known each other. Moving in together was a huge deal.

Ella frantically tried to figure out how to backtrack just as the door to Logan's room burst open and his family filed in, hurrying over to the bedside, demanding to know how he was feeling.

Embarrassed, Ella tried to disentangle herself from Logan's grip to get out of his bed, but he just held her tighter.

"Ella."

She looked back at him, and knew he could see her fear that she'd screwed everything up.

Amusement twinkled in his eyes. "I'll move in with you."

Ella sensed his family sharing glances behind her, but she couldn't turn her gaze from Logan's sparkling green eyes as he added, "And since we're diving right into serious, Ella, will you marry me?"

Ella could feel her mouth opening and closing silently, but she couldn't seem to say anything.

"I'm sorry I don't have a ring," Logan added, sounding nervous. "But as soon as I get out of this bed…if you say yes…"

Someone nudged her from behind. "Say yes," Becky whispered.

"Yes," she breathed.

And then Logan was kissing her and his family was laughing and crying and congratulating them. And she knew, she just knew, that coming to Oakville to find a serial killer had been the best decision she'd ever made in her life.

* * * * *

MILLS & BOON®

Why shop at millsandboon.co.uk?

Each year, thousands of romance readers find their perfect read at millsandboon.co.uk. That's because we're passionate about bringing you the very best romantic fiction. Here are some of the advantages of shopping at www.millsandboon.co.uk:

* **Get new books first**—you'll be able to buy your favourite books one month before they hit the shops

* **Get exclusive discounts**—you'll also be able to buy our specially created monthly collections, with up to 50% off the RRP

* **Find your favourite authors**—latest news, interviews and new releases for all your favourite authors and series on our website, plus ideas for what to try next

* **Join in**—once you've bought your favourite books, don't forget to register with us to rate, review and join in the discussions

Visit **www.millsandboon.co.uk**
for all this and more today!